SEAL

SEALs of Coronado

PAIGE TYLER

ISBN-10: 1543141412
ISBN-13: 978-1543141412

Cover Design by Gemini Judson, Cover Gems

Editing by Wizards in Publishing and RVP Editing

With special thanks to my extremely patient and understanding husband, without whose help and support I couldn't have pursued my dream job of becoming a writer. You're my sounding board, my idea man, my critique partner, and the absolute best research assistant any girl could ask for!

Thank you.

PROLOGUE

Al Qanat, Northwestern Iraq near the Syrian Border

YOU'VE GOT TO BE FRIGGING KIDDING ME."

At the words, Navy SEAL Trent Wagner turned to the door of the small mud brick hut where he and the other members of his Team—Logan Dunn, Nash Cantrell, and Dalton Jennings—had been waiting for the past several hours. Dalton didn't recognize the four men who'd walked into the building, but one look at his Teammates' faces suggested they definitely did. And none of them seemed happy to see the newcomers.

So much for this mission being simple.

Three days ago, ISIS fighters had captured a group of American and European missionaries providing aid to refugees in northern Syria and hustled them across the Iraqi border to Al Qanat. ISIS claimed the missionaries were, instead, spies and planned to spend a couple of days using the hostages to film a few propaganda videos to improve recruitment before beheading them and posting the clips on the Internet for the world to see. Trent supposed the terrorists probably thought that would convince people ISIS was still a force to be reckoned with, even as the rest of the world kicked their ass.

The plan had been for Trent and his Team to slip into the encampment on the edge of Al Qanat and rescue the missionaries at precisely 0200 hours, when there'd be the least number of guards. They'd sneak in, deal with the guards, and rescue the missionaries without engaging in any serious fighting, then load the missionaries on a helicopter outside the city before going back to laser designate the ISIS camp for an unmanned Predator bombing run.

If everything had gone according to plan, the entire mission would be over and done with by 0300 hours. It was nearly 0430 now.

Trent and the guys had been getting ready to move in when the secure satellite text message had come through, telling them to hold their position and that a second special operations team was being brought in to join them. That hadn't made a lot of sense to any of them. This mission had been planned from the get-go for a small, four-man team. Why the hell would

Special Operations Command suddenly think they needed additional resources?

"Should have known," Logan muttered. Tall with dark blond hair, he had blue eyes, which were currently filled with disdain. "The only agency SOCOM would be willing to hold up a rescue mission for is the CIA." He glared at the four men who'd just come in. "Let me guess. ISIS wasn't lying when they claimed one of the missionaries is a spy. You slipped a CIA plant into Syria posing as a missionary, didn't you?"

None of the CIA guys said a word, but they looked as pissed as Logan, Nash, and Dalton did.

"Now might be a good time to remind you that I'm the new guy in this platoon, Logan," Trent said. "Maybe someone could tell me what the hell is going on and make some introductions?"

Trent had been on Coronado's SEAL Team 5 since graduating from BUD/S, but only recently moved over to Logan's platoon. While Trent loved the guys in his former platoon like brothers, he hadn't minded the change. Logan's platoon had a reputation for doing some crazy missions. That was cool with Trent. The way he figured it, if you were going to get shot at for a living, you might as well have fun while doing it.

Logan pointed at one of the men on the other side of the hut, a stocky guy with dark, curly hair. "Say hello to Joe—he runs this SOG team."

Trent had to stop from whistling out loud. SOG—as in Special Operations Group. That explained a few things. The CIA's special operations soldiers, they were responsible for carrying out military missions on behalf of the nation's most secretive intel agency. Trent had never run into any of them before, but he knew there was no end to the kind of mischief they could get into. Except for hostage rescue. That wasn't typically something they wasted their time with. Which meant Logan was probably right about them being here to save one of their own.

That also explained why the air was tense with the possibility of violence even though they were supposedly all on the same team. Rumors going around SEAL Team 5 had it that Logan embarrassed the shit out of the CIA— and SOG in particular—about a month ago, when he'd slipped a Russian defector out from under their noses in order to help rescue his new girlfriend who'd been kidnapped. Trent didn't know all the details, but, regardless, Logan, and by extension, his platoon, weren't on the best of terms with CIA SOG.

But all that was in the past, or at least it should be. There were a lot of hostages in deep trouble who were depending on their working together. They could all be professionals here.

"Don't worry about what to call the other three," Logan added with a snort. "I've come to think of them as Moe, Larry, and Curly. Though now that I think about it, I guess that would make you Shemp, wouldn't it, Joe?"

Okay, so much for everyone being professional.

"Logan, stick a sock in it," Nash ordered before glowering at Joe and his guys. "Everyone else, take it down a notch."

Nash's words didn't seem to have much of an effect on Logan or the SOG guys. They looked like they were about two seconds from throwing haymakers.

"Nash is right," Trent said. "I know there's some bad blood between you guys, but we don't have time to screw around. We barely have an hour until sunrise. If we don't get this rescue op going in the next few minutes, we're going to have to wait until tonight, which means those hostages will have to live through another day in this hellhole—if they lived that long. We need to move now, and we need to move together."

Something unspoken passed between Logan and the leader of the SOG team, and, a moment later, both men nodded.

"Okay, we'll do this together," Joe said. "What's the plan?"

Alongside his Teammates, Trent carefully made his way across the dark, quiet courtyard toward the main building within the ISIS encampment. With no moon visible, it was nearly pitch black. Despite that, he and his guys hugged the wall of the brick building as they headed for the back entrance. The place used to be a food and medical supply warehouse for the small city before the ISIS soldiers had taken it over to house their troops and equipment as well as turn it into a makeshift prison for their captives. They didn't need a lot of space for the latter. ISIS rarely let their prisoners live long enough for it to matter.

If the intel they had was right, there'd be only three guards. At this time of night—or morning, rather—one would be on duty while the other two slept.

Once Trent and his Team were inside, he

and Nash would deal with the three guards while Dalton and Logan headed for the prison cells. In the meantime, Joe and his SOG guys would come in through a side entrance and take up a position between the cells and the main part of the warehouse where the majority of the ISIS fighters were sleeping. It was risky, but their job was to make sure reinforcements couldn't get to the back of the building to help the guards—or interfere with the rescue. If the SOG guys hadn't shown up, Trent and Nash would have done that job. The last thing any of them wanted was an unarmed hostage getting shot by some ISIS soldier who heard a noise and decided to see what it was.

When they reached the heavy steel door, Trent grabbed the handle and gave it a careful pull. As expected, it didn't budge.

He pressed his ear to the door, listening for any sound of movement from within, but didn't hear anything. Swinging his MP5 submachine gun over his shoulder, he turned off his night vision goggles and flipped them up. Making a motion to warn the others, he pulled the Tec Torch breaching tool out of his tactical vest and shoved the end against the door, right at the place the deadbolt would be located. The Tec Torch was about the size of a small flashlight and contained a thermite cartridge that burned at a temperature of over five thousand four hundred degrees when lit. The jet of molten metal that'd come out of the end of the breaching tool would only last for about two seconds, but during that time there wasn't anything it couldn't slice through.

Trent checked to make sure Nash and the other guys were looking away so the flash of the blazing metal wouldn't burn out their NVGs then flipped the arming switch, pressed the fire button, and averted his face to protect his eyes.

The tool erupted in his hand, making a sound not much louder than a hissing cat. He moved the tool down the door a little, working by feel and experience, pulling on the handle at the same time. The torch cut the deadbolt away in less than a second.

Trent yanked the door open, moving aside as the guys slipped past him. He tossed the spent and now useless torch aside and flipped down his NVGs then followed Nash into the small room where all three guards were sleeping. Unfortunately, the ISIS soldiers were already awake and reaching for their AK rifles.

One of the terrorists opened his mouth to sound a warning to his ISIS buddies, but Trent and Nash fired their silenced weapons and dropped all of them before the men could make a sound. He and Nash hesitated only long enough to grab a ring of keys on a nail pounded into the wall by the door before heading out of the room.

They found Dalton and Logan halfway down the hallway, their weapons pointed in the direction of the main part of the building. Logan motioned at several of the doors, giving Trent a nod. He nodded back, quickly getting to work figuring out which keys on the big ring went to which lock.

Five open doors later, they had their eight missionary hostages and were ready to move out. Seven of the men were in fairly good shape. A little bashed, bruised, and weary, but mobile. The last man—who was almost certainly the CIA plant—had been badly beaten and was unconscious. Nash quickly checked him for major injuries, but in their current situation, he couldn't do much for the guy. Nash and one of the other hostages draped the man's arms over each of their shoulders and headed down the hall toward the door.

Logan gave Joe and the other SOG agents the signal over the radio, letting them know they had the hostages and were moving out. The CIA guys had to hold their position long enough to ensure the hostages were clear and this mission was essentially over.

Then a barrage of automatic weapons fire sounded from the direction of the main part of the warehouse, and Trent realized this mission was just getting interesting.

"We're cut off," Joe said in Trent's earpiece, the soft *pop-pop-pop* of the SOGs silenced weapons audible over the countless number of AK-47 assault rifles being fired. "Get the hostages out of here. We'll slow these bastards down."

Trent looked at Logan, waiting to see what the senior ranking SEAL would say.

Logan motioned toward the hostages then in the direction of the back door. "Nash and Dalton, get them out of here and to the extraction point." He glanced at Trent. "Let's go save these damn spooks before they get themselves killed and blame it on us."

Nash and Dalton immediately hustled the missionaries out of the building while he and Logan ran toward the shooting.

There were so many green tracer rounds blazing through the wide open central area of the warehouse that it nearly flared out Trent's NVGs. But he didn't need crystal clear vision to figure out what was going on. In the green shadows of his goggles, he made out four shapes huddled down behind heavy equipment racks. The CIA guys were returning fire, but they were pinned down and heavily outnumbered. They couldn't stick their heads out long enough to properly defend themselves.

Trent pulled a frag grenade out of his waist pack and yanked the pin. Nodding at Logan, he flung it toward the heaviest concentration of ISIS soldiers then ducked into the hallway after his Teammate. A split second later, the grenade exploded, rocking the building and echoing in his ears.

He and Logan darted back into the main room, immediately laying down fire. The grenade had taken out a lot of ISIS fighters, but there were more left to take their place, and they were fanatical enough to die for their cause instead of turning tail and running.

In the end, it came down to training and discipline. Trent, Logan, and the SOG agents were simply better at hitting what they aimed at.

"We'll cover you," Logan told Joe over the radio. "But move your ass!"

The SOG guys might not like Logan, but they weren't going to argue with him at the moment, not when their asses were on the line. The CIA agents moved fast, covering the distance between their side of the room and the entrance to the hallway in seconds while Trent blazed through a full magazine of ammo keeping the bad guys ducking.

Logan tossed one of his grenades, and they were all halfway out the back door before it exploded. They didn't slow down, leaping over the wall surrounding the courtyard and heading into the desert toward the extraction point.

"We're out of the building," Trent called over the radio.

The words had barely left his mouth before the soft drone of the Predator's props churned through the air somewhere overhead. Seconds later, there was a sharp crack as two five-hundred pound bombs hit the warehouse behind them. Trent didn't bother looking back to see what was left. There wouldn't be much.

The missionaries and the unconscious CIA spy were already loaded on the waiting Air Force CV-22 Osprey and the huge tilt-wing rotors beginning to pick up speed by the time Trent and the rest of the guys got there. Nash and Dalton were standing at the rear loading ramp, weapons ready and faces anxious.

"Finally!" Nash shouted to be heard over the revving engine of the big aircraft that was half helicopter and half plane. "We were just about to go back to look for you."

Logan chuckled as they ran aboard the air transport and scrambled for seats among the hostages. "We would have been here sooner, but Joe and his guys slowed us down."

The engines revved more loudly as the aircraft leaned forward and took off, getting them airborne and away from the area quickly. Trent glanced at Joe and his SOG warriors, expecting a sharp retort to Logan's jab.

Joe laughed and shook his head. "It's not our fault we don't run as fast as you SEALs. You have more practice running away from shit."

Trent tensed along with everyone else as they waited to see what Logan would say, but his Teammate laughed.

"Good one," Logan said. "Did you come up with that on your own?"

Trent laughed. Everyone else did, too, including the SOG guys.

"But, seriously," Joe said, looking at Trent, Logan, Dalton, and Nash each in turn. "We owe you, and that's something we're not going to forget. You ever need our help with anything, all you have to do is ask."

Then Joe and his guys were up and moving over to check out their spy, who was being tended to by an Air Force medic up near the front of the plane.

"Might be nice having the CIA owing you a favor," Logan said. "Never know when it might come in handy."

CHAPTER
One

San Diego, California

WHAT AM I GOING TO DO WITH TWO WEEKS OF leave?" Trent asked, flopping back on the big sectional couch in his apartment and sipping his beer. "All we do in the SEALs is travel, travel, and travel some more. I sure as hell don't want to travel somewhere on vacation."

On the other end of the couch, Nash was nursing his beer and clearly paying more attention to the Padres playing on the big screen TV than the conversation. "No one is saying you have to go anywhere on leave, Cowboy. They're saying you have to burn some of it."

Trent snorted. Most of his new platoon had taken to calling him *Cowboy* because he grew up in Texas. Not exactly the most creative nickname he'd ever heard.

"I don't want to take leave at all," he grumbled.

Nash shook his head. "You have to. You've got what—a hundred and ten days' worth of leave on the books? Headquarters is really good letting us stockpile leave because we deploy so frigging much, but sooner or later, they're going to make you take some of it."

That was true enough.

"Guess I'll update my Netflix account and binge watch some shows then."

Although that might be more complicated than it was for most people since Trent rarely watched TV, and when he did it was usually football, baseball, or basketball.

Nash dragged his gaze away from the game to look at him. "Isn't there anyplace you've wanted to visit? Some exotic foreign locale? Maybe a natural wonder like the Grand Canyon or something. I happen to know for a fact that you have the money to go anywhere you want because you live like a frigging monk."

Trent made a face. "What are you talking about? I go on a lot of dates."

Well, maybe not a lot, but he went out. Just usually not with the same woman more than a couple of times. It was hard having a steady relationship when you were a SEAL.

"I'm not talking about sex," Nash said. "I'm talking about this place."

As if to prove his point, Nash motioned around at Trent's sparsely furnished apartment. Okay, maybe it was kind of Spartan. He'd simply never worried about what the place looked like because he wasn't around enough to care. When he wasn't deployed on a normal rotation, he was in standing at the operations officer's desk volunteering to go out with any Team that needed an extra body. Besides, what more did a guy need than a couch, a television—even if he rarely watched it—and a comfortable bed?

Trent swigged his beer. "Okay, I see your point, but it'd be kind of dull to go somewhere on vacation on my own."

Nash grunted in what sounded like agreement. Like Trent, Nash hadn't exactly been very lucky when it came to finding a steady relationship. Being a SEAL had its advantages if you were looking for a one-night stand, but if you were looking for something more than that, it could be a liability. No woman wanted to wait around for you to get back from your eighth deployment of the year—if you came back at all.

"Why not go visit your family back in San Antonio, then?" Nash asked.

Trent grimaced. "I'd like to, but it's... complicated."

"How so?"

Where did he start?

He leaned forward and set his beer on the coffee table then rested his forearms on his thighs. "I grew up on a ranch outside San Antonio. My parents still run the place with lots of help from my brothers and sisters, which is something they remind me about every time I go back there. I'm the only one who doesn't live within ten miles of the ranch, the only one not married, and the only one without any kids."

It was Nash's turn to wince. "Mom and Dad not so thrilled with your career choice, huh?"

"Yeah." Trent shrugged. "I mean, they're proud of me and all, but they're not shy about saying they'd prefer if I got out of the SEALs and moved back to the area. You know, settle down and start a family. I love them, but it's hard to deal with the constant nagging when I visit."

"Okay, that definitely explains why you're not hyped to run home and catch up with the family," Nash said. "What about friends? Aren't there any high school buddies you want to hang out with? Your parents wouldn't have to know you're in town."

Trent grabbed his beer, draining half of it before answering. "I do have a buddy I've known since we were kids who I wouldn't mind catching up with."

"So, go see him."

"I'm not so sure that'd be a good idea," Trent said. "He's had some trouble with the law."

"Ah," Nash said in understanding.

Trent stared at the TV, not watching the game but remembering the kid who used to laugh all the time and charm his way out of trouble with that sugar-sweet smile and fast-talking mouth. Then the image changed to a tired-looking teenager with dark circles under his eyes and clothes hanging off a gaunt frame.

"I'm not sure where his life derailed, but Marco fell in with some bad people during our junior year of high school," Trent explained. "I stuck with him anyway. I mean, we were friends, and I wasn't going to write him off, regardless of what he did. Unfortunately, I couldn't keep him from walking away from me."

"What happened?"

"He dropped out of school partway through our senior year, and by the time I left for Navy boot camp, Marco had gotten involved in selling drugs as well as doing them and got a five-year sentence for possession with intent to distribute. He got out in less than that, but ended up right back in the life and doing a second stint in prison for simple possession. My parents mentioned that he's out now, but still..."

"I get it," Nash said. "You'd like to see your best friend, but he has a prison record."

"That's part of it," Trent admitted. "It probably wouldn't do my security clearance any good if the investigators found out I'd been hanging out with a convicted felon with a drug history. Even if that weren't an issue, I'm not sure what the hell I'd talk to Marco about now. To say we've grown apart is an understatement."

Nash didn't answer.

Trent stared at the baseball game, wondering what the hell the whole conversation they'd had said about his life. He loved his family but never went home to see them, his best friend had gotten into trouble and disappeared from his life, and when his boss told him to take some time off from an insane work schedule, there was no place he wanted to go.

He was still thinking about that when the doorbell rang.

"That had better be Dalton with the damn pizza," Nash grumbled. "I'm frigging starving. We should have gotten delivery instead of letting him pick up the pies."

Trent got up and opened the door without

looking through the peephole. He expected to see Dalton standing there with two pepperoni pizzas in hand, but instead it was a beautiful, dark-haired woman. All he could do was stare. Damn, she was seriously cute.

"Trent?" she said.

Not only did she have the face of an angel, but she sounded like one. Well, at least he imagined that was what an angel sounded like. He was so mesmerized it took him a minute to realize she was regarding him questioningly, like she was afraid he didn't recognize her.

He was pretty sure he didn't. He never would have forgotten a woman this stunning.

Trent was about to say as much, but then caught himself as her big brown eyes, silky dark hair, perfect tanned skin, and her pert little nose tickled a memory buried way back in the recesses of his mind. Little by little, he drew the memories out, until he thought that maybe he did know her—maybe.

"Lyla...is that you?" he asked hesitantly.

He still wasn't completely sure he was right. If this woman was indeed Lyla Torres, then she'd definitely been drinking a lot of milk since he'd seen her last because something had sure done her body good. She was all sexy curves and long legs.

And if the woman was Lyla, then every law of serendipity in the universe had been severely violated, because he and Nash had just been talking about her brother, Marco. What were the chances of that?

The gorgeous woman standing on his doorstep nodded, confirming she was in fact the younger sister of his best friend. Or at least the man who used to be his best friend.

"It's me." She smiled. "Can't you tell?"

Trent returned her grin. "Yeah, but you've changed—a lot."

He tried to be good and keep his eyes from sliding down her body to take another peek, but he mostly failed at that. Lyla didn't seem to notice. Laughing, she stepped close to wrap her arms around him.

"You've changed a lot, too," she said, giving him a squeeze. "You were always well built, but I can't even get my arms around you now. Where did all these muscles come from?"

Trent automatically wrapped his arms around her, inhaling deeply as he buried his face in her thick, dark hair. She smelled absolutely intoxicating. "Better diet, I reckon."

Lyla was two years younger than he was, which was why he'd never made a move on her back in high school even though he'd always thought she was cute. Their ages just hadn't worked out quite right. Besides, the bro code had made her completely off- limits. There was no way he would have tried to date his best friend's younger sister. That would have been ten different levels of wrong.

"What are you doing here?" he asked, finally pulling back to look at her. Damn, a man could get seriously lost in those dark eyes of hers if he wasn't careful. "Don't get me wrong," he added quickly, not wanting to offend her. "But it's not exactly a short trip out here from San Antonio."

She stepped back a little, too, but kept her hands on his forearms. She had nice long, graceful fingers with beautiful rounded nails.

"I came out here to see you. Well...to ask for a favor. Your mom mentioned to my mom where you lived, so I thought I'd take a chance and see if you were home. I know I should have called or something first, but..." The smile faded from her eyes to be replaced with worry. "It's just that I'm in trouble and could really use your help."

Trent opened his mouth to reply, but Nash beat him to it.

"Of course, we'll help you." Nash stuck his head out the door, flashing her a grin. "You don't even have to ask. Helping beautiful damsels in distress is what we do."

"We?" Lyla said, ignoring the over the top compliment and instead giving his SEAL Teammate a dubious look.

"This is Nash," Trent said before his buddy could open his mouth and say something embarrassing. "He's a friend, and on the same SEAL Team with me. He's right, though. If you're in trouble, we'll do anything we can to help."

She sagged with obvious relief and took a deep breath like she'd been holding it the whole time.

"Come on in," Trent said.

Lyla nodded her thanks and slipped past him and Nash into the apartment. Beside him, Nash followed her with his gaze then gave Trent a look.

"What were you saying about not knowing where to go on leave?" he asked softly. "Like she isn't enough reason to go home."

Trent closed the door with a shrug. "She's my best friend's younger sister, which makes her kind of off-limits."

Nash considered that. "I guess, but still…"

Trent ignored him and led the way over to the couch. Lyla was obviously in some kind of trouble. There was no way he was going to make a move on her when she was vulnerable.

He grabbed the remote from the table and turned off the TV. "Can I get you anything to drink?"

Lyla shook her head as she sat down. "I'm good, thanks."

Taking a seat on the other leg of the sectional, Trent leaned forward and rested his forearms on his thighs. "What kind of trouble are you in, Lyla?"

"It's not me," she said. "It's Marco. He's missing. I think he's gotten himself into something really bad."

Trent cursed silently, his mind immediately going to the obvious place. Marco was a convicted felon with a history of using and selling drugs. If he was missing, there was probably a good reason.

Lyla held up her hand. "I know what you're thinking. That Marco went to prison—twice—and that he's a drug dealer and a junkie. And you're right. But that was in the past. I know it sounds lame, but it's true. Marco fell in with a bad crowd, and he let them lead him to places he never should have gone. After he got out of prison this last time, he put that life behind him and got clean. He's an artist now and earns a good living making and selling metal sculptures. He has a permanent showing in a gallery in San Antonio and several traveling exhibits that display his art all over the Southwestern United States and Mexico. He's becoming really well known."

Trent had a hard time imagining the guy he used to know being any kind of artist, especially a metal sculptor.

"But?" he prompted when Lyla didn't continue.

Lyla bit her lip. "Ten days ago, he didn't show up for a lunch date we'd made. I got worried, so I went over to his place. The door had been kicked in, and there were signs of a struggle. I haven't heard from him since."

From where he stood in the center of the living room, Nash exchanged looks with Trent. No doubt his Teammate was thinking the same thing he was. Just because Marco had tried to turn his back on the life that had dragged him down didn't mean people in that world were ready to let him walk. It sounded like someone from Marco's past had come calling.

"Did you call the police?" Trent asked.

Lyla laughed, the sound bitter and scornful at the same time. "Yeah, but the cops aren't interested in looking into the disappearance of an ex-con like Marco. They didn't dust for prints or anything. All they did was look around and write a report."

"What about his parole officer?" Nash wondered. "He recently got out of prison, so I assume your brother has one."

"He has one, but participating in the program he was on in prison this last time—the one where he learned how to cut and weld metal—meant he only has to see his parole officer once a month. Marco isn't due to meet with the guy for another two weeks, and I'm hesitant to say anything to him early because I'm afraid he'll revoke my brother's parole and the cops will put a warrant out for his arrest." She grimaced. "His parole officer isn't too thrilled with the way the new program allows my brother to travel all over the place, especially down to Mexico. I'm worried about Marco, but I don't want to risk putting him back in jail—or destroying his new career. I can't do that to him."

Trent frowned. "What do your mom and dad think?"

"I haven't told them," she admitted. "And they aren't involved in Marco's life enough to realize it themselves. Dad won't let him come to the house anymore. If Mom wants to see Marco, she has to go to his apartment."

Well, that had to suck for Lyla. Trent knew

that most people in their hometown considered Marco a complete screwup and too worthless to bother with. Yet Lyla had stuck with him. Now he was missing, and the police didn't seem interested in finding him. She couldn't tell his parole officer for fear of getting him in trouble—if he was alive—and she couldn't tell their parents any of it.

"Why did you come here, Lyla?" he asked quietly. "What do you think I can do for you that the police can't?"

Her eyes misted and, for a moment, he thought she might burst into tears. But then she squared her shoulders and took a deep breath.

"I'm not sure what you can do," she said. "But you were always Marco's friend, and you stuck with him even when his life started going in the toilet. My brother has burned every other bridge he's ever made, but I was hoping the one he had with you might still be solid. I thought maybe you could come back to San Antonio and help me look for him." She swallowed hard. "I'll understand if you don't want to. It's a long way to go for a friend you haven't seen in years, especially one who has completely screwed up his life. But you're the only person I could think to turn to. If you say no, I'm on my own."

Trent gazed at his best friend's little sister. Lyla had changed a lot in the years since he'd seen her, but the one thing that hadn't changed was how much she cared about her older brother. She was worried about Marco and wasn't going to let this go. If Trent didn't help her, she'd look on her own. No matter how much trouble that got her into.

On the other side of the coffee table, Nash lifted a brow. "You said you didn't have anything to do with two weeks of leave. Looks like you do now."

Trent supposed that was true. He didn't have a clue what was going on with Marco, and at the moment, he guessed that didn't really matter. He'd go and stick his nose into the situation and see what he could learn. If nothing else, at least he could keep Lyla from getting into any trouble herself. Marco had let some bad people drag him down. There was no way in hell Trent would let those same people get their hands on Lyla.

CHAPTER
Two

Y OU CAN DROP ME OFF AT THE NEAREST HOTEL AND
pick me up in the morning," Trent said.
"Between the long flight and having to wait
for our bags, it's too late to start looking for
Marco tonight."

Lyla glanced at the clock on the dash as she
started her Toyota RAV-4 and groaned. She
couldn't believe it was after two in the morning.
So much for getting a chance to look for Marco
the moment they got here.

"Don't be silly," she said to Trent as she put
the SUV in gear and backed out of the space
she'd parked in when she'd dropped it off that
morning at the airport. "I have an extra bedroom I use as an office to grade papers and pre-
pare my lesson plans. There's a futon in there
you can sleep on. It might not be the most comfortable thing in the world, but at least it won't
cost you an arm and a leg like the hotels around
here."

He nodded. "As long as you're comfortable with the idea of my crashing at your place. I don't want you to feel obligated to put me up."

"You flew all the way out here to help me find my brother—I am obligated." She smiled. "And as far as being comfortable with your staying with me, of course, I am. I've know you since I was five years old."

As she headed for the exit to the airport's long-term parking lot, the clock on the dashboard reminded Lyla once again how long it had taken to get back to San Antonio. The flight itself was barely more than four hours, yet it had taken them over twelve to make the trip. She'd tried not letting her frustration show during that time, but she wasn't sure she'd succeeded. It wasn't Trent's fault it had taken so long, any more than it was his fault they'd lost so much time picking up their bags. The flight from San Diego had been stuffed to the gills, and although she and Trent had small carry-ons, they'd been forced to check the bags anyway.

That was merely one of the things that had delayed them. Getting Trent onto a flight had been the first challenge. Airlines seemed to have a problem with people who showed up at the airport at the last minute. Trent actually had to buy his ticket online first. Then they'd needed to change her ticket. She'd originally intended to fly back to San Antonio tomorrow since she'd had no idea how long it would take to convince Trent to help her. Unfortunately, she hadn't bought the kind of ticket that could be changed easily. The woman at the counter had given her holy hell about moving to an earlier flight, but luckily Trent—and his credit card—had solved all their problems. Of course, now she owed the big Navy SEAL an even bigger debt of gratitude. Then again, if he could find Marco and get her brother out of whatever mess he was in, she was going to owe Trent a lot more by the time this was over with.

Lyla glanced at the man beside her, the man she'd gone all the way to San Diego to find. She'd known him since they were both kids, so she'd been sure she would recognize him the second she saw him. And she had, in a way. His hair was still as dark blond as ever, and his eyes were still that vivid blue that made it nearly impossible to speak whenever she looked at him. And that smile—the one that had always made her heart speed up—was still the same, too.

Trent had definitely changed a lot since the last time she'd seen him, though. He'd always been tall and fit in high school, but she swore he'd grown at least three inches since then and had packed on a lot more muscle. He didn't look bulky like a powerlifter or anything. No, he was more like a lean, strong, jungle cat. She supposed all the stuff she'd read in the news lately about SEALs being amazing was true because Trent definitely looked ah-mazing.

Considering the way he'd agreed to fly out here to help look for her brother, Trent might be more remarkable than most. He hadn't so much as paused to debate the fact that her brother was a criminal in the eyes of most of the world. When she'd asked Trent for help, he'd simply said yes. There weren't many guys who'd do that.

"You said something about grading papers and writing lesson plans," he said as she headed north away from the airport. "You're a teacher, then?"

She nodded, abruptly realizing they'd spent the entire flight from San Diego talking about nothing but Marco and the people she thought he might be involved with. The notion of talking about anything else—like her personal life—hadn't entered her mind.

"Yeah," she said. "I teach fifth grade at the elementary school in Shavano Park. It's a really good school system with great kids. I'm on summer vacation right now, which is a really convenient time for my brother to go missing, all things considered."

"I know Shavano Park," he said. "Do you live there, too?"

She shook her head. "I wish. But no. I can't afford to live there on a teacher's salary. I live in Stone Park. It's only a few minutes north of the school, but the rent is easier to handle."

Thankfully, Stone Park was also only about fifteen minutes from the airport. Her long day was finally catching up to her. She was beat. Trent, on the other hand, looked wide awake. Maybe it was a Navy trick or something.

When they got to her apartment building, Trent carried her bag and his up the three flights of stairs to her place like they were nothing. She flipped on the lights the moment they walked in the door. The two-bedroom apartment was on the small side, but she loved coming home after a tough day in the classroom anyway.

Trent set down the bags on the floor near the loveseat, his gaze taking in the plants she lovingly cared for, the framed photos of family and friends, and the many knickknacks she'd collected.

"This is nice," he said.

"Thanks." She gave him a smile. "I purposely rented a place on the lower end of my budget so I could save money and do some traveling during the summers."

She would have said more, but a yawn snuck up on her. She hid it behind her hand then gave Trent an apologetic look.

"Sorry about that."

"Don't be. We can talk tomorrow." He grinned. "Right now, I think it's time we get you into bed."

The words had her pulse skipping a beat. If Trent wasn't a guy she'd known since elementary school, she would have thought he was flirting with her. Since she had, she was simply going to chalk up the line to exhaustion on both their parts.

"Good idea." She turned, motioning with her hand for him to follow while she tried to hide her blush. "Come on. I'll show you where everything is so you can crash, too."

He followed her through the small apartment while she pointed out the kitchen, bathroom, and second bedroom. Then she grabbed some sheets and a pillow and showed him how the futon converted into something that slightly resembled a bed.

"If you're hungry, feel free to raid the

fridge," she added. "I'm not sure there'll be anything in there you'll like, but you're welcome to check it out."

He chuckled. "If you have ketchup, I'll eat cardboard."

She doubted he'd be so agreeable once he got a peek at her collection of Greek yogurt, coconut water, and soy milk. But she'd worry about that tomorrow. They could stop at the grocery store while they were running around looking for Marco.

Lyla left Trent making up the futon while she headed to the bathroom to get ready for bed. Normally, her nighttime ritual took at least thirty minutes, but she was too tired to go through the full routine. She got her makeup off, brushed her teeth so her mouth wouldn't taste like the bottom of a birdcage in the morning, and pulled on her long, threadbare University of Texas at San Antonio sleepshirt then called it a night.

When she opened the door, she found Trent leaning against the wall in the hallway outside the bathroom wearing tight khaki shorts and a snug-fitting T-shirt with some kind of surfing logo on the front of it. She wasn't quite sure what it was because, well, there were so many muscles to look at instead. Damn, he had the most amazing body she'd ever seen.

She ignored the flutter in her tummy and jerked her thumb at the bathroom. "It's all yours."

Giving his shoulders, biceps, and long, muscular legs one more lingering glance, she turned and headed for her bedroom. She didn't get more than a few feet before she spun back around to face him again.

"Everything happened so fast today that I didn't get a chance to say thank you." She gave him a sheepish look. "You didn't have to use your vacation time to come back here with me, but I'm glad you did. So, thanks...okay? It really means a lot to me."

"You're welcome." His mouth curved up at the edges. "I only hope I can help you find your brother."

Lyla returned his smile. It was crazy to think Trent could show up and simply fix everything just like that. She wasn't naïve. She knew her brother was likely in some serious trouble. But having someone as strong and confident as Trent here gave her hope. At the moment, that was all she could ask for.

"We'll find him together," she said. "I'm sure of it."

CHAPTER
Three

T HE NAME ON THE ELEGANT SIGN ABOVE THE DOOR
said, *The Show Piece*. Even if Trent hadn't
known the fancy glass and metal building
in the Southtown art district was a gallery, he
would have figured it out. The place simply had
that artsy look to it.

"So, this is the place Marco shows his stuff,
huh?" Trent asked Lyla as they got out of her
SUV.

Knowing his old friend's recent criminal
history, Trent had had certain preconceived
notions about the place. He'd expected a grit-
ty looking building with graffiti on it in a run-
down part of the city. This gallery, however,
screamed upscale and expensive.

Lyla smiled as they walked toward the door.
"I told you he's been doing well since turning
his life around. One whole wing of the gallery
is set aside exclusively for his work. They sell at
least a couple pieces a week, and his traveling

exhibits do even better."

Trent decided then and there he needed to stop with the preconceived notions. He hadn't talked to Marco in a long while, so maybe it was time he admitted his friend actually might have changed his life for the good.

It was better than thinking the worst of his friend at every turn.

Trent couldn't keep his eyes from locking on Lyla's butt as she walked through the door he held open. She was wearing a flowy colorful top and tight jeans she looked damn good in. Made him wonder what she would look like out of them.

Okay, now his jeans were getting tight.

As they slowly made their way through the gallery, he cursed silently and forced himself to focus on the little cubicles filled with framed paintings and small sculptures mounted on pedestals. Trent had never thought about it one way or the other, but after passing through half a dozen of the displays, he came to the conclusion he wasn't cut out for art appreciation. That was okay since it just gave him more time to appreciate Lyla—and there was certainly a lot to appreciate.

She'd been worn out last night when they'd gotten to her place, but she'd still managed to look gorgeous. Rather than make her old college sleepshirt look like it had seen better days, she'd made it seem like a provocative fashion statement.

I'm so attractive, I make threadbare look good.

And how. If the situation had been different, he probably would have flirted with her a little. But the timing was all wrong for that. Not only was Lyla worried about her brother, but so was he. So he'd stuffed his libido back in his tight Navy-issue swim trunks along with his hard-on and gone into the bathroom to brush his teeth. Then spent most of what was left of the night fantasizing exactly what Lyla looked like under that shirt.

While Lyla hadn't seemed nearly as exhausted this morning, she was still clearly preoccupied with worry over Marco. They'd made a few general plans on the flight from San Diego last night. The first item on the agenda was to talk to the last person who'd seen Marco, the manager at the gallery that sold his art, Dana Olson. Lyla said she'd talked to the woman briefly a few days after her brother disappeared and hadn't learned much. Trent wanted to talk to her, if for no reason than to find out what Marco had been up to in the days before he'd gone missing. If they were lucky, the woman might know more than she realized.

After that, the plan got a little vague, re-volving around a general concept of checking out the people from Marco's criminal past who might know something about his disappear-ance. The reason that part of the plan was so iffy was because neither he nor Lyla had a clue who those people might be or where to find them. They'd have to make that part up as they went. Then again, maybe Dana Olson could point them in the right direction.

Lyla led him past several people casually pe-rusing the artwork as well as a couple talking to a dark-haired woman who worked there about buying a painting that covered nearly a whole wall toward the back of the gallery. When they got there, she paused to point out the section dedicated to Marco's work.

Trent couldn't help but stop and stare in surprise. The guy he'd known back in high school hadn't possessed an artistic bone in his body. Marco's idea of beauty had pretty much started with a woman's butt in a pair of tight jeans and ended with a 1969 Boss 429 Mustang. Apparently, his friend had changed since then.

There were eight large metal sculptures po-sitioned around the exhibit area. Trent found himself wandering around them, marveling that the man he knew had made these things. Although each of the pieces was totally unique, Trent could see the consistency of style that connected all of them to the same artist. Some were incredibly realistic, like the one showing a dragon with its wings extended lifting a huge Texas longhorn from the ground, while others were designed simply to provoke an emotion, like the weeping willow that made Trent feel sad merely by looking at it.

But whether they were realistic or abstract, they were all powerful and beautifully crafted. The metal shaping, welding, and polishing that had gone into each of the pieces must have taken weeks—maybe months—to accomplish. Trent didn't know anything about art, but he knew amazing when he saw it, and Marco's works were nothing short of amazing.

"Wow," he breathed.

Lyla's lips curved. "Yeah. That's the same reaction most people have the first time they experience Marco's stuff. You can see now why I said he's left his old life behind. This is who he is now."

Taking Trent's hand, she led him past the sculptures and out of the main gallery down a short hallway. Stopping outside an open office door, she knocked lightly then stepped into the small room.

"Dana?" she said. "Do you have a second?"

A slender blond woman in her early thirties looked up from her computer. At the sight of them, she immediately jumped to her feet and came out from behind her desk. "Lyla! Tell me you're here with news about Marco?"

One look at the dark circles under the woman's green eyes and the concern on her face made Trent think Dana was more than simply the gallery owner who sold Marco's work. He was right. The moment Lyla shook her head, Dana's eyes filled with tears. Yeah, there was something else going on for sure.

"We stopped by hoping you might have heard something," Lyla said.

Dana's gaze shifted to him curiously. "We?"

Lyla glanced at him. "This is Trent Wagner, an old friend of Marco's. He's helping me look for my brother. Trent, Dana Olson, the owner of the gallery."

The curiosity disappeared from Dana's eyes to be replaced by hope. In his line of work, Trent had seen that expression on enough desperate people's faces around the world to recognize it. Dana had no clue who he was, but he was someone trying to help, and that was worth latching onto.

"It's nice to meet you," she said, lifting a manicured hand to wipe a tear from her cheek. "I just wish it wasn't under these circumstances."

"Me, too," Trent said. "I'm guessing you and Marco have more than a business relationship. Am I right?"

Lyla looked at him in confusion even as Dana gave him a sad smile.

"Is it that obvious?" she asked. "I thought I was doing a better job of hiding it."

Lyla blinked. "You and Marco are a couple?"

Dana let out a sigh then nodded. "Sit. Please."

Closing the door, she gestured to the antique armchairs in front of the big wooden desk before taking a seat behind it again.

Like the rest of the gallery, this room was decorated with photographs, paintings, and various sculptures. Trent couldn't help noticing one particular small metal piece occupying a position of honor on Dana's desk. It depicted a naked woman sitting artfully on an equally naked man's lap. It was stylized and modern and didn't look like anything he'd ever seen before. It looked pretty damn sexy for a hunk of steel, too. The fact Dana had put it in a place where she could see it every time she looked up from her computer told Trent a lot.

"We've been involved for over a year," Dana explained. "Since shortly after he got out of McConnell State Prison this last time. Marco came in with a piece he'd made while in there. I have no idea how he got the thing out, but he was completely honest about his criminal background and asked me if I thought it was something someone would buy. I told him no."

Trent frowned. "It wasn't any good?"

That same small, sad smile tugged at her lips again, her gaze going to the naked couple on her desk. "It was too good, too perfect to be the first piece he sold. I told him I wouldn't sell it, but that I'd give him enough money to live on for a week so I could see whether he had it in him to make something equally special." She looked at Trent. "Obviously, he had. That's when I set him up with an apartment and a studio and began to help him develop his brand. He took me out to dinner to celebrate the night he sold his first piece. We've been seeing each other ever since."

While Dana wasn't that much older than Marco, she must be wealthy if she was able to pay for his apartment and studio. A cynical part of Trent wondered if she was just in it to make money off Marco. From what he'd seen, his old friend was certainly talented enough to make an unscrupulous person a lot of money. But Dana really seemed to care about Marco.

Beside him, Lyla looked stunned. "Why didn't Marco ever tell me?" she asked Dana. "Why didn't you? I've been in here at least a dozen times, and neither of you ever hinted you were seeing each other."

Dana gave her an embarrassed look. "That was Marco's idea. He was worried if it got out that I was having a relationship with a convicted felon, it might make people look at me differently and end up affecting the gallery. He didn't want that, and I'm ashamed to admit I went along with it. I shouldn't have. It was only after Marco disappeared that I realized how stupid I'd been." She gestured around them. "None of this is as important to me as Marco is, and if I had to sell it tomorrow to have him back safe and sound, I'd do it in a second."

Lyla leaned forward, reaching out to take Dana's hand and give it a squeeze. "You're not going to have to do that. We're going to find Marco, and he'll be fine. Then you can tell anyone you want you're together."

Dana nodded, tears glistening in her eyes again.

"Lyla said you were the last person to see

Marco before he disappeared," Trent prompted. "Did anything unusual happen?"

Dana frowned. "Something happened but it wasn't unusual. People from Marco's past were always showing up, trying to cause problems, wanting to bum money for drugs or trying to drag him back into the life. When I stopped by his studio the night before he disappeared, I interrupted an argument between Marco and one of those people."

"Do you know what they were arguing about?" Trent asked.

"Not the details," Dana said. "They stopped talking when they realized I was there. But I heard enough to figure out it had something to do with the protection Marco received while he was in prison."

"Protection?" Lyla asked.

Clearly, she didn't understand what that meant. But Trent did, and he didn't like the sound of it.

Dana shrugged. "It's not something Marco ever talked about. He never wanted me around that part of his life. But over time he let enough slip for me to figure out someone powerful had been watching out for him while he was in McConnell, making sure no one bothered him."

"Any idea who that person is?" Trent asked.

He wasn't an expert on the criminal mind or how protection in a prison worked, but he was smart enough to realize if someone had taken care of Marco in the joint, they hadn't done it out of the goodness of their heart. It was possible Marco's disappearance had something to do with him owing a debt to that person and not wanting to pay.

"I have a pretty good idea," Dana said.

"You do?" Lyla asked, clearly stunned. "Who?"

Dana got up and walked over to one of the large filing cabinets in the corner. Opening the top drawer, she retrieved a folder then came back and sat down. She flipped through the folder, taking out a slip of paper and sliding it across the desk for Lyla and Trent to see.

"I think it's this man—Archie Cobb." She pointed at what looked like a sales receipt with a really large dollar figure at the bottom. "He came to Marco's first big showing and bought one of the pieces. Marco got upset, and it almost turned into a fight right here in the gallery. When I asked him later why it bothered him so much that Cobb had bought one of his pieces, he said something cryptic about already owing the man enough."

Trent glanced at Lyla to see her expressing

the same interest he was. This definitely sounded like something they should check into.

"Don't suppose we're lucky enough to have an address on this guy, Cobb, do you?" he asked Dana.

"I'm afraid not. The man paid cash for the piece—a large lion with the horns of a bull and the tail of a dragon—and he had someone pick it up with a truck, so he never left an address." Dana's brow furrowed. "That's not a problem, is it? You can find Cobb on your own, right?"

Lyla looked doubtful, but Trent nodded. He actually had a good idea where he could turn for this kind of information. Granted, it was a longshot, but it might work.

"I think I know someone who can help," he said. "I'll call him as soon as we're done here."

Dana relaxed a little at that, but Lyla only eyed him curiously.

They spent a little while longer talking to Dana about other occasions when Marco's past had come calling. There was one guy in particular who'd shown up a lot.

"You're talking about Tim Price, right?" Lyla asked.

Dana nodded.

"Who's Tim Price?" Trent asked.

"The jerk who got Marco involved in drugs

back in high school," Lyla muttered. "He convinced Marco to smuggle drugs across the border, and they both ended up doing time together at McConnell. Tim Price is nothing but trouble."

"Tim acts like his friend," Dana added. "But I get the feeling he has no interest in ever letting Marco get his life back together."

Trent scowled. "Any idea what all these people want with Marco, beyond the apparent desire to keep him down in the toilet with them?"

Dana shook her head.

After that, the conversation shifted into a discussion of how close Dana and Marco had become and how she was trying to help him move beyond the criminal events in his past.

"There's a lot of interest in Marco's art in Europe." Dana smiled. "We're thinking of going to France and starting a second gallery over there once he's fully off probation."

It all sounded very heartwarming and casual, as if Lyla and Dana had forgotten Marco had been missing for over a week and was probably in a crapload of trouble. But Trent wasn't going to remind them. If they wanted to stay positive, he didn't intend to point out the obvious.

Before they left, Dana made them promise they'd keep her up to date on anything they

learned, good or bad. Lyla nodded and promised she would, reminding Trent that neither
she nor Dana was as naïve as the conversation
moments ago had implied. They knew the situation was bad. They simply chose not to dwell
on it.

"Were you serious about knowing someone who can track down Archie Cobb, or were
you saying that to make Dana feel better?" Lyla
asked when they were back in her SUV.

"I was serious. There are some people in San
Diego who might be able to help. I'm just not
sure if they will."

After digging his phone out of his pocket,
Trent scrolled through the contacts, stopping
when he reached Chasen Ward, the newly pro-
moted chief petty officer of his platoon. He hit
the button to call the man before he could think
better of it.

Chasen picked up on the second ring.

"What's up, Cowboy?" he asked before Trent
could get a word out. "Nash told me you went to
San Antonio to help out a friend who's in trouble. Everything okay?"

Well, that made things a little easier. The
fact Chasen knew why he was in Texas meant
he wouldn't have to waste time explaining
everything.

"Everything's fine, Chief," Trent said. "I called because I could use some help."

There wasn't even a second's delay. "Shoot. Whatever you need."

"A little while ago, Logan and Nash mentioned you and Haley got involved with that hacktivist group—*The People*—and knew how to get in contact with them."

"Logan and Nash talk too much," Chasen muttered. He didn't sound very amused.

"Yeah, probably," Trent agreed. "Is it true? Can you contact them? If you can, I need a big favor."

"What kind of favor?" the chief asked, not necessarily saying he'd do it, but not shutting him down either.

"I'm trying to find a guy named Archie Cobb. He's some kind of criminal here in the San Antonio area, and we think he might be involved in the disappearance of my friend, Marco Torres. I was hoping you could talk to these hacker friends of yours and see if they can find out how to track down Cobb. If it helps, I'm almost certain he's in the drug business. There's also a man named Timothy Price who's involved. The two names might be connected."

There was silence on the other end of the line for a moment. "Are you about to get yourself into deep shit out there, Cowboy?"

Trent opened his mouth, ready to lie in order to help his friend, but then changed his mind. "Possibly. But I don't have a choice. Marco may be in serious trouble. If I don't help him, nobody will."

More silence followed, and Trent held his breath.

"Okay, thanks for being honest with me," Chasen finally said. "I'll get my friends to dig into Archie Cobb and see what they can find. I'll ask them to look into Timothy Price, too. Give me an hour or two. These people can be difficult to reach."

Trent let out a sigh of relief. "I can do that."

"I'll call you as soon as I learn something," Chasen promised. "Watch your back out there, okay, Cowboy? If things get out of hand, call me. I'll get some of the guys out there to watch your back."

"Thanks, Chief. I will."

"Hackers?" Lyla asked. "Navy SEALs have hackers on speed dial?"

Trent chuckled. "Something like that. They'll see if they can find an address on this Cobb dude, but until then, you feel like grabbing some lunch?"

Lyla didn't have to think about it very long.

"Lunch sounds good. If we're going to check out bad guys who are involved in dealing drugs, I should probably have more on my stomach than a few spoonfuls of yogurt.

Trent wasn't sure of that logic since a full stomach rarely made much difference when it came to dealing with bad guys, but he nodded anyway. "Lunch it is."

"San Diego has some great Mexican restaurants, but sometimes I seriously miss the Tex-Mex flavors you can only get in San Antonio." Trent crunched into the big taco he'd ordered and chewed then let out a moan. "Oh man, that's good."

Lyla couldn't help laughing. In some ways, Trent was like a really big kid. She absolutely loved that about him. A lot of guys would have been too worried about acting cool to moan over their food like Trent did. But the big, strong Navy SEAL she'd brought back from San Diego with her didn't seem to care about any of that. It was like he didn't realize how gorgeous he was, which was hard to believe. She'd have thought a few hundred women would have pointed that out to him by now. Then again, maybe the women out in San Diego didn't know how incredible he really was. If Trent lived in San Antonio, she had no doubt he'd have plenty of women interested in telling him exactly what they thought of him. And Lyla didn't have a problem admitting she'd be one of them.

She quickly refocused her attention on the burrito she'd gotten, digging into it with her fork and hoping she hadn't been staring at him too blatantly. She'd done that a lot since showing up on his doorstep to beg for his help.

She scooped some of the shredded chicken covered with onions and chilies into her mouth, almost moaning a little herself. Wow, this was really good. She'd never been to Maria's Café on Nogalitos Street before, but it was a nice place to eat. Casual, too. Kind of like having lunch at a friend's house instead of a restaurant.

"Since you're so close to the border in San Diego, you must go to Mexico and eat real Mexican food all the time, right?" she asked in between bites.

It was safer to engage him in polite conversation about food than to think too long about how much fun it was to stare at the guy on the other side of the table. This wasn't a date. Trent was here to help find her brother. That was it.

He was off to a good start, too. The conversation they'd had with Dana earlier had finally given her hope she might be able to get somewhere in her search for Marco. They had a name, and now that the hackers Trent's SEAL buddies knew were trying to track down Cobb, they might actually learn something useful. She refused to let herself think too much about what a man like Cobb might have done with her brother. She and Trent were going to talk to Cobb, and that would lead her to Marco. She was sure of it.

"Actually, I don't get across the border all that often, maybe once a year at most," Trent said in answer to her question. "I travel a lot with my job, and to tell the truth, I'm usually not in the mood to get out much when I'm home."

Lyla supposed she could understand that. After a hard week of teaching at her elementary school, there were times she was so exhausted she couldn't bother to get off the couch for the entire weekend. She supposed Trent's job could be like that, too.

That was when she realized she didn't have a clue what his job entailed. Yeah, she knew he was in the Navy SEALs, and of course, she heard the news talking about SEALs going up against ISIS in Syria. But she really had no idea what SEALs actually did on a daily basis.

"This is probably going to sound horrible since I'm a teacher and supposed to know everything about everything," she said as she sipped her iced tea. "But what exactly do you do for a living? Besides traveling a lot, I mean."

Trent chuckled as he polished off his taco and started in on another. "Don't feel bad about not knowing much about SEALs. When we do our job right, nobody is supposed to have a clue we've been there, much less what we've done. And most of the stuff you see in the news is wrong."

"Okay. So, what's the real story, then?"

He licked some sauce off his thumb. "SEALs are trained to conduct small team operations anywhere in the world. We're able to move into and out of the objective area by sea, air, or land—hence the name SEAL. We do covert reconnaissance, hostage rescue, counterterrorism operations, direct action against small, high value targets. Stuff like that."

Lyla had a general idea what that stuff meant, but she got the feeling Trent was glossing over the details and purposely making light of what he did for a living. She was certain everything he'd described was dangerous as hell.

"So, you're like Army Rangers, right?" she asked.

He reached for his iced tea. "We're part of the larger special forces community, like the Army Special Forces and the Rangers, but also Marine Force Recon and Air Force Pararescue. We all work together under the same Special Operations Command, but we're better than the rest of them."

Lyla laughed. "Not bragging are you?"

He grinned. "It's not bragging if it's true."

She shook her head. Guys had to be competitive about everything, didn't they? She waited for him to say something else about the kind of work he did in the SEALs, but when he didn't, she realized she'd probably gotten as much out of him on the subject as she was going to.

"You said that SEALs work in small teams," she said. "How small? More than just Nash, right?"

"We occasionally go out as two-man teams, but typically, it's in groups of four to eight. SEAL platoons normally have sixteen people in them, but there aren't many missions that require all of us at one time."

Sixteen sure as heck didn't sound like a lot of people to her, not if they were doing some of the scary stuff Trent had mentioned. She'd want to have a couple of hundred people with her—or a couple of thousand. Safety in numbers was her motto.

"Doesn't it get scary?" she asked. "Going out there with so few people, I mean. What if something goes wrong?"

"The people in my Team are really well trained. Some of the best special operations warriors in the world." He winked. "We don't get into trouble. We cause trouble for other people."

She laughed. Like he'd just said, it wasn't bragging if it was true. "After seeing you and Nash together, I get the feeling you're really tight with your Teammates."

He nodded. "Yeah. They're like my second family. In some ways, they're more family than my real family. I spend almost every waking moment with them, and we go through a lot, so we're close."

"Is that why the guy you called agreed to help you track down Cobb?"

"Pretty much," he admitted, starting on his third taco. "Chasen got involved with a group of hackers a few months back, and I figured if anyone could help us out, it'd be them."

Lyla wanted to ask what the story was behind that, but then another thought struck her.

"If Archie Cobb grabbed Marco, do you think there's any chance he's still alive?"

She told herself not to go there, but she'd be lying if she didn't admit the thought had been floating around in the back of her head from the moment she'd heard the man's name.

Trent set his taco down and wiped his fingers on his napkin then reached across the table to take one of her hands in his. "We're not doing this, Lyla. I know it's natural to worry about your brother, but the fact is, we simply don't have enough information to do anything but make up stuff. And trust me when I say this: the human mind can come up with some pretty crazy stuff if you let it—far worse than reality will ever get. So, we're going to stop thinking about what might be, and instead, focus on the one thing right in front of us—finding Cobb and seeing what he knows."

"And then?"

"Then we'll take it from there, one step at a time. There's no use worrying about the next step because it's a waste of energy."

While that made sense, it was easier said than done. "I guess that's your SEAL training coming out, huh?"

Trent shook his head. "No. That's a lesson everyday life taught me. Worry about what's in front of you and let the other stuff take care of itself."

They fell silent while Lyla went back to eating her burrito and Trent finished his taco then turned his attention to the black beans and rice that had come with it. Trent was right. She had to stop thinking about the bad things that might happen to Marco and instead, focus on talking to Cobb.

"I never knew you wanted to be a teacher," Trent said, loading his fork with more beans. "Back in high school, I mean. I swear I remember you taking all kinds of math and science classes because you wanted to go to med school."

She smiled, knowing he'd purposely changed the subject so she'd stop worrying about Marco, and because she was thrilled beyond all reason Trent had actually paid enough attention to her in high school to remember the classes she'd taken, as well as what she'd wanted to do with her life back then.

"I originally did go to the University of Texas at San Antonio for a microbiology and immunology degree," she admitted. "But by the second semester, I realized I was making a huge mistake."

He frowned. "What convinced you?"

She scooped up another forkful of burrito mixture, remembering the moment she'd decided to change majors like it was yesterday. "Don't get me wrong. It wasn't anything monumental or dramatic. My roommate had family come in for the weekend, and her younger brother and sister—twins—were stuck in the common room doing their homework the entire time. They were in the fifth grade and totally bummed they couldn't go out and have fun like everyone else. I ended up helping them do their homework instead of going out, too. My roommate felt terrible, but it turned out to be the best thing that ever happened to me. I'd never had that much fun in my biology classes, and it convinced me what I really wanted to do with my life was teach elementary school. I changed majors before the next semester and never looked back."

Trent regarded her thoughtfully. "Funny the way things work out sometimes, isn't it?"

"Yeah, I guess so." She sipped her tea. "Like who ever could have imagined you'd be back in San Antonio staying in my guest room after us not seeing each other for nearly eight years?"

He chuckled. "That definitely goes in the category of something I never would have imagined happening."

"Not that you mind though, right?" she asked, the words coming out a little faster and more frantic than she'd intended. Had that sounded just as pathetic to him as it had to her?

Trent didn't seem to notice. "I wish the situation that had brought me here was different, but I can't say I'm upset about the opportunity to spend time with you."

She opened her mouth to thank him, but the words got stuck as she realized he was gazing at her with an expression on his face you didn't normally see on your brother's best friend. The funny thing was, this wasn't the first time she'd seen that expression. Now that she thought about it, she realized he'd regarded her the same way when he'd opened the door of his apartment in San Diego, then again when she'd walked out of the bathroom last night wearing nothing but her old college sleepshirt.

She decided she really liked it when he looked at her that way.

"This may or may not come as a shock to you, but I had a huge crush on you back in high school," she said softly.

Lyla felt her face warm the second the words were out of her mouth, and she could have smacked herself for saying them. It was like she couldn't shut up when he looked at her sometimes. What the hell had she been thinking?

Trent's blue eyes glinted. "Yeah, I knew. And while I never would have admitted it back then, I definitely had a crush on you, too."

She blinked. "You did? I never knew." She bit her lip. "Do you think things would have been different between us back in high school if we'd been the same age?"

His brow furrowed as he considered that. "Maybe. But to tell the truth, while the age difference was certainly a complication, the fact your brother was my best friend was the bigger issue. Marco probably would have come after me with a two-by-four if I ever treated you as anything other than his baby sister."

"I was never his baby sister," she pointed out.

"No, you definitely weren't," he agreed with a smile. "But you were his sister, and he was very protective of you. When he started screwing up his life with drugs and crap, that never changed."

Lyla opened her mouth to ask him if he was worried about Marco coming at him with a two-by-four when he figured out Trent was sleeping in her spare bedroom, but before she could get the words out, his phone rang, interrupting her.

He pulled his cell out and glanced at the screen. "It's Chasen."

Thumbing the speaker button, he placed the phone on the table between them. Lyla looked around, wondering if this was the best place to take this call. But they were at the end of the lunchtime rush, so there wasn't anyone else in this section of the restaurant. She supposed it was okay. Or at least Trent must have thought so.

"What's up, Chasen? Did you learn anything about Cobb?"

There was silence on the phone speaker for a second, and then a man's deep voice answered. "Yeah, I learned some stuff about Cobb. Enough to ask what the hell you're getting yourself into, Cowboy. When Nash said you were helping an old friend from high school, I didn't think you'd be going up against one of San Antonio's biggest crime bosses."

"Is that what Cobb is?" Trent asked, not ruffled in the least.

"Yeah, and he's got a reputation for being a cold-blooded, vicious bastard. You sure you don't need a few of us to fly out there for backup?"

Lyla stared at the phone, not sure if she was more shocked to learn Cobb was a huge crime boss, or that Trent's SEAL buddy seemed ready to jump on a plane and help him deal with the aforementioned crime boss.

"Thanks, but I'm good, Chief," Trent said. "You got an address on this guy?"

CHAPTER
Four

I'D FEEL BETTER IF YOU STAYED IN THE CAR," TRENT said as they sat in the front seat of the parked SUV in front of the nightclub off Interstate 37. "I have no idea how many of Cobb's people are in there at this time of the day."

"Forget it," Lyla said firmly. "I asked you to come to Texas to help find Marco, not risk your life. If you're going in there, I'm going, too."

She grabbed her purse and hopped out of the SUV without waiting for a reply. Trent ground his jaw as he got out and met up with her when she came around the front of the car. Her logic made no sense. He was going into a place owned and operated by a known crime boss, which would obviously put his life at risk. Her going in with him wouldn't change that at all. It would just put her life at risk as well.

But he doubted Lyla was likely to listen to him if he told her that. He got the feeling she did whatever she thought was right, regardless of the danger. Something else he couldn't help but admire about her.

When they reached the front door of the club, Trent glanced up at the big red brick building and the enormous metal chain links that spelled out the name of the club, and let out a snort.

Chains.

Clever, he supposed.

He looked at Lyla. "Sure you don't want to change your mind? I seriously think it would be better if you waited in the car."

Lyla shook her head and reached for the handle. Trent beat her to it, pulling open the door. He was a little surprised the place wasn't locked up. It wasn't even 1400 hours—two o'clock—yet. A place like this probably didn't open for business until eight.

The inside was dimly lit, and it took a second for Trent's eyes to adjust. The club was larger than he expected. Chasen had said Cobb fronted his criminal operations through a string of nightclubs across south Texas, stretching all the way from Houston to El Paso, with the one here in San Antonio being the biggest. The chief hadn't been exaggerating. This place was big enough to hold at least a thousand people.

While the club would be a great place to sell

drugs out of, Chasen seemed to be of the opinion that Cobb used it strictly as a way of laundering money made from selling meth, heroin, and cocaine through his other venues. Trent supposed that made sense, too. Cobb wouldn't want to draw too much attention to his main base of operations.

As he and Lyla weaved their way through the tables and crossed the glass and metal dance floor, Trent noted they'd carried the chain motif inside. Long lengths of heavy gauge anchor chain were strung from the ceiling, some ending in lights that were mostly off at the moment, but others holding up large gilded cages. Trent didn't have to exercise his imagination much to figure out what those cages held during normal business hours.

"We're not open yet," a loud male voice boomed.

Trent turned to see a guy in his mid-thirties stacking bottles of booze on the shelves behind the long bar that took up the entire far wall.

"Club opens at eight," the man told them. "You'll need to come back later."

"We're not here to party," Trent said. "We're here to talk to Archie Cobb."

The guy's whole demeanor changed, his face turning seriously unfriendly. "Mr. Cobb doesn't take meetings without an invitation, and I'm pretty sure you're not the kind of people who'd make the list."

As if on cue, three other men walked out of a doorway near the far end of the bar and came toward them. Beside Trent, Lyla inhaled sharply.

One man was tall and thin with red hair, his face rough from years of hard living, while the other two were a little shorter, but bulkier, the kind of guys you'd see working out six days a week at the gym and at night working the door of a club.

"What are you doing here, Lyla?" the thinner man asked, his face curious as he looked first at her then at Trent.

"We came to talk to Archie Cobb," Lyla said, her voice steadier than Trent would have thought it'd be. "Though, I guess I'm not all that surprised to see you here, Tim. You and Cobb strike me as the kind of people who'd hang out together."

Tim. As in Tim Price, the guy who'd been in prison with Marco.

"Mr. Cobb isn't here right now, and he wouldn't see you if he was," Tim said. "You should leave."

Without waiting for a reply, Tim turned and

headed toward the same door he'd just come out of.

"I think we'll stay and wait for Mr. Cobb to come back," Trent said. While he deliberately kept his tone light, he couldn't keep from sounding a little pissed off. "I can't speak for Lyla, but I'm a witty conversationalist. I'm sure your boss would regret the opportunity if he didn't get a chance to talk to me."

Tim stopped and turned back around to look at him, ignoring Lyla completely. "And who are you?"

Trent's mouth twitched. "I'm a friend of Lyla's—and Marco's."

The corner of Tim's lip curled up in a sneer. "Marco never did have very good taste in friends." He glanced at the two bruisers with him. "Escort Lyla and her friend out. Make sure they understand it'd be in their best interest if they don't come back."

As Tim walked away, the two goons headed straight toward Trent. He casually stepped in front of Lyla. This was exactly why he hadn't wanted her to come in here with him.

"Trent?" Lyla asked uncertainly as the two men moved onto the dance floor and closed the distance between them.

Trent had no choice but to ignore her as he

focused all his attention on the approaching threat. He could tell from the way they walked that the men were used to physically intimidating and overpowering people based on pure size and strength. Neither of them seemed to possess the speed or agility that made him think he had to worry about any kind of martial art skills.

One of the men moved slightly slower than his buddy, favoring his left leg a little, like he'd injured it recently. Trent went with his instincts and took several more steps to that man's side, forcing both guys to slow and change direction a bit. As expected, Bum Leg did exactly what Trent wanted, dropping back behind his partner so they could come at him one at a time.

"Look, fella," the guy in front said. He had a big forehead and brooding brow that reminded Trent of a Cro-Magnon. "This is going to hurt, no matter what, but it's a matter of how long you want to be in the hospital, so don't make this hard on us."

"I certainly wouldn't want to make things difficult for you," Trent said, giving Cro-Magnon a cool smile as he took another step toward him.

When Cro-Magnon reached out to grab his shoulder, Trent didn't try to evade him.

Instead, he grabbed the guy's hand and shoved it aside, lunging forward at the same time. Cro-Magnon's eyes widened in alarm, but it was too late for him to do anything as Trent slammed his forehead into the bridge of the big guy's nose. The crunch was shockingly loud as Cro-Magnon's nose broke, but the noise was relatively soft in comparison to the shout of pain the guy let out as he staggered backward into his buddy. Bum Leg stumbled, almost falling, but Trent had no time to deal with him yet. While the fight looked like it was over for Cro-Magnon, Trent couldn't take the chance. In one smooth move, he reached out and got his hands on the man's shoulders, yanking him forward at the same time he viciously brought his right knee up into the man's crotch.

Cro-Magnon's bloody face immediately turned pale, and he collapsed. Trent brought his knee up again, this time connecting with the man's jaw. There was another crunch of bones, and Cro-Magnon flopped to the floor in one big, unconscious heap.

Trent stepped over the man, advancing on Bum Leg. The guy had already recovered his balance and was reaching behind his back for something. Trent had no doubt it was a weapon of some kind. Apparently, he'd decided he didn't like the odds of dealing with Trent hand to hand.

Bum Leg was smarter than his friend, backing up a bit to give himself time to get his weapon out, but his bad knee was slowing him down. Trent used that to his advantage, moving to close the distance between them quickly. But not before the man pulled out a large .45-caliber automatic and swung it in his direction.

Behind Trent, Lyla shouted a warning, but again he had to ignore her as he threw himself forward to grab Bum Leg's arm before the guy could line up a shot. The guy took a swing at Trent with his left hand. It was an awkward shot at best, and Trent blocked it easily. Then he pivoted his weight to his left foot, freeing up his right for a kick. Bum Leg twisted his body as well, probably assuming Trent was going for another nut shot. Trent didn't blame him. If he'd just seen his friend take a knee to the balls, he'd be guarding his groin, too.

But Trent had no intention of going for the man's crotch. He had another target in mind—Bum Leg's bad knee.

Bum Leg groaned when Trent's heel connected with it. The man dropped to the floor, clutching his leg and grimacing in pain. Trent took advantage of the distraction, ripping the man's .45 away from him then smacking him in the temple with the butt of the hand grip.

Trent was jacking the upper receiver back to make sure a round was in the chamber when he heard a distinctive metal clanking sound coming from the direction of the bar. He spun, raising the heavy automatic and aiming by pure instinct, lining it up with the bartender, who'd just yanked a shotgun out from behind the bar and pumped a shell into the chamber.

"The chances of you hitting me with a shotgun blast from all the way over there is pretty damn low," Trent said as he sighted his gun on the man's forehead. "But I can absolutely guarantee I'll put a big ass .45 round right between your eyes, no fucking problem."

"Who the hell are you? And what the hell do you want?"

Trent glanced over to see Tim had come back and was looking more pissed off than before.

"I already told you," Trent said. "I'm a friend of Marco's. Like Lyla said, we're here to talk to Mr. Cobb."

"Then perhaps you should turn around so you can talk to him," a deep voice said from behind Trent.

Beside him, Lyla immediately spun around.

Trent moved more cautiously, sliding to the side so he could keep an eye on both the bartender and Tim, as well as Archie Cobb. The stocky crime boss in the expensive silk suit wasn't alone. Marco was with him.

Marco Torres had changed a lot since Trent had last seen him. He was still lean, but he didn't look as gaunt as a couple of years ago. Lyla was right about her brother not using anymore. Marco looked a hell of a lot older than he should, though, gray already salting his short, dark hair and showing up in the scruff along his jawline.

But, above all that, the biggest change was the sadness in his friend's eyes. He had the gaze of a man who had done a lot of stupid stuff and disappointed a lot of people.

"Marco, where have you been?" Lyla asked, even though the fact her brother was standing next to a crime boss pretty much answered the question.

"I was down in Mexico," Marco said. "Doing some work."

"For him?" Lyla asked, glaring at Cobb.

"It's complicated," Marco answered.

"Complicated?" Lyla demanded, nearly trembling with anger. "Is that what you call it when you decide that selling drugs for this man is more important than moving forward with your life? Is that what you call it when you decide to turn your back on me and on Dana and on all the people who love you?"

"Lyla," Marco pleaded softly, the little light left in his eyes completely fading at the anger and accusation in her voice.

"Forget it!" she snapped. "I have no idea why I bothered caring about you when you can't be bothered to care for yourself."

Blinking back what looked like tears, Lyla hurried for the exit, not looking at Trent. He followed anyway, shaking his head as Marco took a step forward, attempting to slow his sister. The look she gave him could have melted steel, and he stepped back, letting her pass.

"Trent?" Marco stared at him in shock as if just now realizing who he was. "What are you doing here?"

"Trying to keep you from making yet another boneheaded mistake with your life, but I can see I wasted my time."

Shaking his head, Trent strode past his old high school friend to catch up with Lyla.

"Can I have that weapon back? It's personal property," Cobb said, stepping in front of him.

Shit. Trent wasn't in the mood to deal with Cobb. Shoot him—yes. Talk to him—no.

Trent brushed past Cobb, forcing the man to step aside or deal with the embarrassment of getting run over.

"If he wants it, he can dig the parts out of the sewer drain outside," he said without looking back. "That's where I plan on tossing them."

Trent caught up with Lyla as she reached the door, and he pushed it open for her. Tears rolled down her face, and she wiped them away angrily.

Fuck. The urge to go back in the club and beat the shit out of Marco was nearly impossible to resist. The only thing that kept him from doing it was the greater urge to get Lyla the hell away from this place.

"Damn him!" Lyla said, pacing back and forth in front of the couch in her living room. It had been over an hour since they'd left Cobb's club, and she was still spitting mad. "I can't believe that after all the times I've had his back, stuck up for him to the rest of the family, paid for his lawyers, Marco is hanging out with that lowlife, Tim Price, and his boss, Archie Cobb."

Out of the corner of her eye, she caught

sight of Trent on the couch following her with his gaze. Lyla appreciated the fact he wasn't trying to get her to calm down like most other guys would. She needed to work off her anger, or she was going to scream. Somehow, Trent sensed that.

When they'd left the club, he'd calmly asked if she wanted him to drive then given her his cell phone to use so she could call Dana because she'd almost lost it after seeing the battery in hers was completely dead. She'd been so worried about her stupid brother, she couldn't remember the last time she'd bothered to charge the damn thing.

Now it looked like all that worry had been a waste of time.

Lyla glanced at Trent as she spun in place to wear a hole in the carpet in the other direction. She couldn't believe how well he was dealing with this. Then again, he'd had a chance to work through quite a bit of his aggression earlier when he'd gotten into that fight at Cobb's club. She still shuddered every time she thought of him taking on those two muscle-bound goons. She'd been shaking in her shoes, but he'd handled those men like it was nothing. He'd never once looked the slightest bit nervous. She wasn't sure if he was incredibly confident or slightly insane.

"I swear, if Marco were here right now, I'd punch him," she muttered.

Trent scowled. "Yeah, well, you might have to get in line."

Lyla stopped pacing to walk over and flop down beside him on the couch.

"I hope Dana's okay," she said. "She was really upset when I called her. It's bad enough Marco screwed me over, but Dana gave Marco her heart, and he stomped on it without a second thought. I don't know how he could do that to her." She dropped her head back on the couch and stared up at the ceiling. "I wish I could understand why he did it. Why, when everything was going so well in his life?"

Trent didn't say anything for a while, and when he finally spoke, his voice was soft, gentle. "Marco headed down this path a long time ago, Lyla. Maybe it's as simple as him not knowing how to find his way back? You tried to be there for him, but at the end of the day, he was the only one who could take the final step. I guess he simply couldn't do it."

Lyla knew he was right, but it still stung like crazy. She'd really believed in her heart that Marco had changed, that he'd gotten his crap together and was finally heading in the right direction. It hurt to think he'd been playing her all along.

"Do you think he's going to end up in jail again?" she asked, even though she already knew the answer.

"Probably," Trent said, then added, "If he's lucky."

She turned her head to the side to look at him. There was a sadness in his eyes she'd never seen before. He was hurting, too, she realized.

Lyla sat up straighter, half turning to face him. "I'm sorry I dragged you all the way out here. You risked your life today, thinking we were helping Marco, and it was all for nothing."

He considered that for a moment then his mouth curved. "It wasn't all for nothing. I got a chance to see you again."

She snorted. "Big whoop. I'm the one who had you going into the club to talk to Cobb. I almost got you shot."

"I get shot at all the time," he said with a chuckle that had her smiling regardless of the insanity of his words. "Trust me, it's much more fun going through it for a beautiful woman than for some guy calling out orders over the radio."

She shook her head, not immune to the fact he'd called her beautiful. "You know that's crazy, right?"

"Maybe," he said with a shrug.

The movement drew her attention to his broad shoulders and muscular pecs flexing intriguingly under his T-shirt. She should have been totally focused on the fact her brother was working for a major drug dealer again and would almost certainly end up back in prison—or worse, dead. Instead, she was thinking about how delicious Trent was. Perhaps she was simply in denial and purposely distracting herself with his sexy body so she wouldn't have to deal with how screwed up her brother was right now.

"Seriously, though." She lifted her gaze to meet his vibrant blue eyes. "You did risk your life for me—and Marco. I owe you. I'm just not sure how you're supposed to repay someone for something like that."

He lifted his hand to gently push her hair back from her face. The brush of his fingers against her skin made her tummy quiver, and she stifled a moan. "And I'm just as serious when I say you don't owe me anything. I came out here of my own free will because I wanted to help you. Having a chance to reconnect with you more than covers the cost of having two big muscle heads try to thump on me."

Again, that was totally crazy, but she wasn't going to try and convince him otherwise anymore. She was simply thrilled he thought it was true, and left wondering at all the ways things could have been different between them.

"So, what are your plans now that we know Marco is safe? Well, alive, at least," she asked. "Will you be heading back to San Diego in the morning?"

A sexy smile slowly spread across his face. "You that eager to get rid of me? What, do I snore or something?"

She laughed. "No. I just figured since there wasn't anything keeping you here, you'd want to head home."

His gaze swirled with sudden heat, making her stomach do that silly quivering thing again. "I wouldn't say there's nothing keeping me here. Besides, I have two weeks' worth of leave to burn so it's not like I have to rush back."

Lyla tried to play it cool, though, with the way he was looking at her, she couldn't keep her heart from beating a little bit faster. "Yeah, no need to rush back, I guess. If you have to take leave anyway. You could spend some time with your family since you're here. Maybe take in a San Antonio Missions baseball game."

"Or I could just hang out with you, making

up for lost time," he murmured, sending her heart rate skyrocketing.

Trent leaned in a little closer as he spoke, looking way hotter than any man had a right to. She wet her lips.

"Yeah, you could do that, too," she said softly.

Lyla didn't expect this thing between them—whatever it was—to go anywhere. She couldn't deny she was very attracted to Trent, and she got the idea he was into her, too. If he ended up staying here for two weeks while on leave, she had no doubt it would be fun, with a good portion of that time likely spent wearing very little or no clothing. But it wouldn't go beyond that. She wasn't the kind of woman who could do the long-distance relationship thing

"Unless..." Trent added, leaning in a little more.

"Unless...what?" she prompted.

Would it be too forward of her to grab him by the shirt and yank him in for a kiss? Probably. Not that she'd ever do it anyway. She didn't have the nerve to pull something like that off. The thought was nice, though.

"Unless you really need your futon back," he finished, moving another inch closer but still keeping his distance. Like he was waiting for her to make a move.

"No," she said, licking her lips. "My futon is yours as long as you'd like to use it. Unless..."

Now it was his turn to be taken by surprise, something Lyla enjoyed seeing more than she would have imagined.

"Unless...what?" he asked, a playful smile tugging at his lips as he moved closer still.

"Unless you can think of someplace else you'd like to sleep," she told him, leaning in this time, hoping he'd take the hint.

He did. His lips were so close to hers she could feel his warm breath on her face. "I can definitely think of someplace else I'd like to sleep."

Lyla was about to ask him to elaborate, but his mouth came down on hers. His tongue slipped inside, teasing hers and making her moan. Trent weaved the fingers of one hand into her long hair, holding her captive as he kissed her deeper. A tingle started just south of her tummy and quickly spread through her whole body.

She slipped her hand into his short hair and thrust her tongue into his mouth, giving as good as she got, pleased when he groaned. The husky sound turned her on more, and she felt a delicious heat beginning to build between her legs.

Lyla released her hold on his hair to slide along his strong shoulders and down over his rippling pecs. Damn, he was built under that shirt. It took a supreme effort of will to keep from yanking it up so she could get her hands—and maybe her mouth—on all those muscles.

She restrained herself—barely—content for the time being to caress his body through his shirt. When her hands got restless and tried to move lower, she dragged them back up and told them to behave. Not that she minded simply sitting there making out with Trent.

That was why she moaned in complaint when he stopped kissing her and pulled away.

"What's wrong?" she asked.

He shook his head, his mouth edging up. "Nothing. I simply don't want to rush this. You don't mind, do you?"

She smiled, secretly pleased for some silly reason that made no sense at all. "I'm good with taking our time. But if we're not going to sit here and make out, what else did you want to do?"

He lifted a brow. "Order pizza?"

She blinked then laughed. She couldn't help it. His response was so completely out of left field she had no other choice.

"You are such a complete...guy," she said. "You know that?"

He grinned and waggled his brows, making her stomach do backflips, twists, and somersaults. "Yeah, I know. Isn't it wonderful?"

CHAPTER
Five

S O, YOU STILL USING THE SEALs AS AN EXCUSE TO avoid getting a real job?" Trent's father reached across the table for the plastic container of carved lunch meat. Though he was nearing sixty, Bruce Wagner was still as fit as he'd been when Trent was a kid, without a trace of gray in his dark hair.

"Bruce!" his mother said in a warning tone as she took a pitcher of her famous freshly made iced tea from the refrigerator. "You stop that right this minute. Your son came all the way home to see us, and I'm not going to let you ruin his visit with your incessant nagging. If you can't behave, you can take your sandwich out to the barn and eat lunch with the horses."

Trent's mouth twitched. At the head of the table, his father looked properly chastised, regardless of the fact he was a huge man of six foot three and his blond-haired wife was barely five feet tall. But no one messed with Darlene

Wagner, not when it came to her children. Not even his dad.

"Something tells me he didn't fly home to Texas to see us," his father grumbled, glancing at Lyla as he began layering slices of turkey and cheese on his sourdough roll.

Trent's mother came over to the table, filling the tall glasses in front of each of them with iced tea. "I know that, Bruce. I might be short, but I'm not stupid. He's home now so I'm not going to complain, and you won't either, if you know what's good for you."

Trent's dad muttered something under his breath but kept any other opinions to himself as he reached for the mayo. Smart man.

Beside Trent, Lyla hid her smile in her iced tea glass as his mother took a seat at the opposite end of the table from his father.

While Trent had intended to visit his family at some point, he hadn't planned to do it today, but Lyla had talked him into it. He would have preferred to stop by her parents and tell them about Marco, but Lyla wanted to put that off for a while. He'd agreed, but only if she came with him to see his parents. Considering he was a Navy SEAL who went up against some of the scariest, meanest bad guys out there, it was embarrassing to need someone to act as a buffer between him and his parents. He'd figured there was no way his father would nag him about getting out of the military in front of Lyla. He was wrong.

Trent hadn't counted on his mother shipping him and Lyla the moment they walked in the door together, though. Heck, she was probably already fitting Lyla for a wedding dress.

As he slathered mayo on his sandwich then took a big bite, Trent looked around the big eat-in kitchen with its modern stainless-steel appliances juxtaposed against old country charm. Despite how reluctant he'd been to come over, he couldn't deny he'd missed his childhood home. He had a lot of wonderful memories of growing up here. With a house full of brothers and sisters, hundreds of acres of land to roam around on, and fields full of horses and cows, he couldn't imagine a better place to grow up on than a ranch.

That said, he still wasn't ready to ditch the SEALs and become a rancher. After leaving San Antonio, seeing other parts of the world and experiencing a lot of different things, running a ranch wasn't for him. He wished his family could understand that.

At the head of the table, his father regarded him thoughtfully. "You never answered my question, son. You planning on getting out of the Navy soon?"

"Bruce," his mother said in a low tone, the warning clear.

"What?" He looked at his wife. "Can't I ask my own son what his plans are for the future? It's not like he can keep doing that SEAL stuff the rest of his life. That's a youngster's game."

His mother sighed in obvious exasperation.

"It's okay, Mom. I don't mind," Trent said. "The answer is no, Dad. I'm not planning to get out of the Navy anytime soon. I enjoy what I'm doing. When I retire, I'll most likely get a job that uses the skills I picked up in the Navy, maybe as an instructor at the school."

His father scowled. "What's wrong with running the ranch? Or are you too good for ranching?"

Trent cursed silently. This was why he hadn't wanted to come over here. Because he knew how the visit would go. He loved his parents to death, and he knew they only wanted the best for him, but his father wasn't above trying to guilt him into getting out of the Navy to help run the ranch. That wasn't to say his mother didn't have her agenda as well. She might be more subtle about it, but she wanted him to move back home, settle down, and give her more grandkids. As if she didn't have enough already.

"No, I'm not too good for ranching, Dad," he said. "I'm just not interested in it. I like being a SEAL. I've told you that before."

About a hundred times.

His father frowned, and Trent prepared himself for the same old lecture about the values of hard work and keeping the ranch in the family. Not that it wasn't staying in the family already since Trent's three older brothers and two older sisters helped run the place.

"So, how did you and Lyla run into each other in San Diego?" his mother asked, interrupting her husband before he could get started.

The question was accompanied by a distinct thud from under the table, and Trent was pretty sure his mother had booted her husband in the shin. His father didn't visibly react—he was too tough for that—but his old man did stick a sock in it, which was all Mom was going for.

"Actually, we didn't run into each other," Lyla admitted, successfully hiding another smile that threatened to slip out. "I went out to San Diego and asked him to come back here and help me find Marco. My brother disappeared for a few days, and I got worried."

His father frowned. "Is Marco okay? I know

he got himself into some trouble a while back."

Understatement there, Trent thought.

At breakfast this morning, Trent and Lyla had discussed whether they should tell anyone about what Marco had gotten himself into. Lyla insisted it wasn't their job to keep her brother's stupidity hidden from the world. Marco had made his decision, and he'd have to live with it.

Lyla's eyes glistened. No doubt she was once again thinking about the road her brother had chosen to go down. Trent instinctively reached out and placed his hand on hers, giving it a squeeze.

"He's okay," she said, then shrugged. "At least as okay as he can be, considering the fact he's let himself get dragged right back in with the same people who got him sent to prison before."

Trent's mother sighed. "Oh, Lyla. I'm so sorry to hear that. We'll be saying a prayer it all works out. I'm just glad you had someone you felt comfortable turning to when you were in trouble."

She gave Trent a pointed look as she spoke, and he could practically see the wheels turning in that head of hers.

Lyla smiled, clearly having no idea his mother was setting her up. "Yes, Trent was amazing.

Not just because he was willing to fly out here on the spur of the moment, but because he had to deal with...well...let's just say some really bad men we ran into while we were looking for Marco."

His mother's eyes widened in shock. His father looked equally concerned.

"You okay?" his dad asked.

"Yeah," Trent said. "It was nothing."

His parents didn't look like they believed him, but they didn't press.

"So, where are you staying while you're in town, dear?" his mom asked as she sipped her iced tea. "Not at a hotel, I hope. We have plenty of guest rooms for you here."

"I'm not staying in a hotel, Mom," he said as casually as he could. "I'm sleeping on a futon in Lyla's guest room."

His mother smiled so big you'd think she won the lottery. She was probably coming up with a list of baby names right now.

As for his father, he was looking back and forth between his wife and Trent, obviously trying to figure out what had just happened. After a moment, his dad's gaze swung to where his hand was still intertwined with Lyla's. It was as if a lightbulb went on because he grinned at his wife.

"Would you like some tomatoes, Lyla?" Mom asked, holding out the serving plate to her. "They're wonderful this time of the year."

Trent shook his head. Oh yeah, his mom was already hearing wedding bells. Man, this was going to be a long two weeks.

"I think your parents are awesome," Lyla said as they strolled along the slowly darkening paths of the San Antonio River Walk a few hours later.

"You might not think that after spending the whole day with them," Trent muttered, still not sure why he'd agreed to his mother's suggestion for the impromptu family reunion with his brothers and sisters the day after tomorrow. He supposed he could put up with his parents' not-so-subtle attempts to talk him into moving back here if it meant getting to hang out with his siblings and their kids.

Lyla laughed. "On the contrary. I'm looking forward to it. I love your mom and dad. I think it's cool how well they get along even though they clearly disagree about things now and then."

Trent had never thought about it that way,

but he supposed Lyla was right. He'd never been sure how his parents kept it together considering they were so drastically different.

"I think they were both on their best behavior today because they were trying to impress you," he said.

"Why the heck would they be trying to impress me?"

Trent reached out and captured her hand, tugging her closer until their shoulders almost touched as they moved along the beautiful network of sidewalks, bridges, and shops lining this section of the San Antonio River.

"Mom has been after me for years to find the right woman and settle down, and after seeing the two of us together today, I think she hopes you're that woman," he told her.

Lyla seemed to consider that then grinned. "I can see why she'd want that. You have to admit, we'd make a cute couple."

He cocked a brow. "Oh really? You think so?"

She laughed and nudged his shoulder with hers as they walked under an arching bridge draped in green ivy, fragrant flowers, and colorful lights. "Sure. Of course, pairing anyone with me would make for a cute couple, so I wouldn't read too much into it."

He chuckled. "I'd like to argue that with you

just on principle, but I can't. You really are frigging amazing."

She looked away like she was perusing the display in the front window of the shop they were passing, but her reflection in the glass gave her away, and he caught her blushing. He wasn't sure why, but he liked making Lyla blush.

As they continued along the walkway, Trent couldn't help but think about last night. All they'd done was hang around her place, eat pizza, and make out some, but he couldn't remember ever having so much fun with his clothes on. Not only was Lyla beautiful, she was also easy to talk to and sexy as hell. He'd never gotten that fired up from simply kissing a woman before. It had taken all his control to keep from stripping off her clothes and his and getting busy right there on the couch.

But he'd behaved himself. This could be the beginning of something special between them. There was no need to rush into anything. Even so, it had been tough falling asleep last night knowing Lyla was in the room across the hall from his wearing nothing but that old T-shirt.

She looked just as delectable in the sleeveless top and floral print skirt she wore today. Not only did the outfit show off her sleek arms, but lots of leg, too. And he'd always been a leg man.

As they slowly made their way over one of the arching bridges that crossed the river, he and Lyla stopped to gaze at the view of the shop lights reflecting off the water.

"Someone told me once that the River Walk looks a lot like the canals in Venice," she said, watching a boat filled with tourists pass beneath them. "Do you think that's true?"

"They definitely have a lot in common when it comes to the canals, the walkways on either side of the river, and the shops," he agreed. "But there's something about Venice that puts it in a class by itself. I don't know. Maybe it's because it has a history San Antonio doesn't. Not that it isn't beautiful here, but there's just a feeling you get when you walk around Venice and realize there are stones along the canals that have been in place longer than the United States has been in existence."

"You've been to Venice?" she asked in surprise.

He shrugged. "Yeah. Some of the other guys on my Team went over to Italy to train with their Navy Raiders—their equivalent of Navy special forces. The training wrapped up early, so my buddies and I spent some time traveling around Italy and doing the tourist thing."

She sighed. "Wow. That sounds so amazing. This is going to sound dull by comparison, but the farthest I've ever traveled is out to San Diego to find you, and we came back before I saw anything beyond the airport and Interstate 5."

He turned to face her, resting one elbow on the bridge as he half leaned against it. She'd put her sunglasses on her head and in the setting sun, her eyes were the color of whiskey. "If you could go anywhere, where would you go?"

She gave him a sheepish look. "Promise you won't laugh."

"Why would I laugh?"

"Because I should probably say France or Italy or Australia or Japan—and I'd love to go to those places someday—but where I really want to go is Disney World."

Okay. He hadn't seen that coming.

"Disney, huh? That sounds cool." He grinned. "Why haven't you gone? Is it the money?"

Lyla shrugged, looking out at the water again. "No, it's not the money. It's just hard to find someone to go with. Most of my friends at the school where I teach are married or in relationships. I guess I've been waiting for the right time—and the right person—to come along."

"I get that. Hell, right before you showed up at my door, I was telling Nash I didn't have anywhere to go on leave for the same reason. It's not much fun going somewhere by yourself."

She laughed, turning away from the water to look at him. "We really are two sorry people, aren't we? We both want to travel to all these exotic places but don't want to go alone."

Trent was about to tell her he traveled enough in the SEALs and had no desire to do it on vacation, but suddenly the idea of going somewhere—anywhere—with Lyla made him rethink that opinion.

"So, let's go together," he said, the words coming out of his mouth before he could change his mind.

Her brow furrowed in confusion. "Go where?"

"Disney World. You said you want to go there, right?"

"Well...yeah, but..." She stopped and thought a moment. "Wait a minute. Are you serious?"

"Of course, I'm serious. I'm a Navy SEAL. We're always serious." He flashed her a grin. "So, what do you say? Do you want to go?"

Lyla stared at him for a second, her mouth hanging open. Before he could tease her about it, she threw herself into his arms, pulling his head down for a kiss. She probably intended for it to be a quick smooch to express her excitement, but the moment her mouth touched his, that went straight out the window.

Trent slipped his tongue into her mouth to tease and tangle with hers as he wrapped his arms around her, pulling her against him so firmly he could feel every one of her sweet curves against his body. Lyla moaned softly, clutching his shoulders and digging her fingernails into his muscles through the material of his shirt.

He glided one hand up her arm then across her shoulder and along her neck, slipping his fingers under her hair to gently massage her scalp while his other hand slid down her back and over the curve of her ass, tugging that most delicious part of her body closer. His cock strained against the front of his jeans.

Lyla sighed against his mouth, her body melting into his, her hips wiggling in slow, tight circles against his hard-on.

It wasn't until a group of college girls walked by, giggling behind their hands, that Trent realized he and Lyla were getting damn close to yanking their clothes off and making out right there on the River Walk. Maybe they needed to take it down a notch before things got any more out of control.

As much as he hated to do it, he slowly pulled back, breaking the kiss and putting a little breathing distance between them. Lyla gazed up at him questioningly, her eyes filled with undisguised lust. Damn, she looked so frigging beautiful right then.

"What's wrong?" she asked.

He lowered his head to trail kisses along her jaw and up to her ear. "Absolutely nothing," he whispered. "But I think we might need to slow down a bit and take a breath, unless you want to end up as the star of our very own YouTube video."

Lyla looked around, as if just remembering they were in the middle of the busiest tourist area in the city. "Oh! Yeah, you're right. That might be a good idea."

Cupping her face in his hand, he brushed his thumb over her lips. "Am I right in assuming that kiss meant you're down with going away together?"

Her lips curved into a big smile. "You are."

"Good." Trent grinned and took her hand. "Come on. We've got some reservations to make."

As they made their way along the path

through the crowd, it occurred to Trent that going on vacation with Lyla at the spur of the moment like this might be one of the most spontaneous—and crazy—things he'd ever done. But he'd learned in the SEALs to listen to his gut, and right now, it was telling him to stop thinking so much and just go with it.

CHAPTER
Six

LYLA COULDN'T STOP GRINNING AS SHE AND TRENT walked into her apartment. They'd spent the whole way back from the River Walk talking about their upcoming vacation, and she was so excited she was having a hard time containing herself.

They actually were going to Disney World.

While she really did want to travel to various exotic places, in the end it had come down to a desire to run around and act like a kid again—and meet Mickey Mouse, of course. She'd been worried Trent would think the entire idea was silly, but he seemed to be as geeked about the trip as she was.

"You're not pulling my leg, are you?" he asked as he followed her over to the couch and sat down beside her.

"Nope. There are hotels at Disney. A coworker and her husband took their kids there a little while ago. There are all kinds of different hotels with different themes."

"Huh," he said, looking amazed and more than a little intrigued. "What kind of themes?"

She kicked off her flip-flops and curled her feet under her. "Since I haven't been there, I don't have firsthand experience, but Amy said they run the gamut from tree houses to ultra-contemporary to ones designed to make you think you're in Hawaii or in the middle of the African plains with real animals all around you."

"Damn. Who knew?" His mouth edged up. "Which place do you want to stay?"

She shrugged. "I'm not sure. We'll have to go online and see what strikes our fancy."

"If we want to go this weekend, we'll have to decide soon so we can make sure we can get two rooms close together."

Lyla reached for her laptop sitting on the coffee table then stopped as what Trent said hit her. After making out last night and that scorching kiss they'd shared at the River Walk, it was kind of silly to think they needed separate rooms.

"You know," she said, sitting back on the couch again, "we wouldn't have to worry about finding rooms near each other if we stayed in the same one."

A sexy grin slowly pulled up the corners of his mouth. "That's true. Plus, rooming together would save money, which would give us more to spend."

"There is that," she agreed softly. "But convenience and saving money aren't the real reason I want us to get a room together."

His eyes smoldered with heat as he leaned toward her on the couch, and his nearness suddenly made her warm all over. "Then, what is your reason?"

She moved closer, too, so they were only inches apart now. "I figured since we'd be spending our days in the parks and our nights in each other's arms, getting two beds would be a waste because I don't plan to let you out of mine."

Lyla wasn't usually this forward with a guy, but Trent was different. Besides being hotter than any other man she'd gone out with, he was a guy she'd had a crush on ever since she was old enough to be interested in the opposite sex. When he'd joined the Navy and left San Antonio, she'd kicked herself for not being bold enough to tell him how she felt. She wasn't going to make that mistake again.

"So, that's how it's going to be, huh?" he murmured tipping his head down until his mouth was a hairsbreadth from hers.

Lyla swore the electricity between them made her body hum, and he hadn't touched her yet.

"Yeah, that's exactly how it's going to be," she said huskily. "And I think we've both known it from the moment we kissed last night."

Trent caressed her cheek, his touch warm on her skin before he slipped his fingers into her hair and tugged her forward to kiss her slowly on the mouth.

"It's what I wanted," he said after a teasing kiss way too short—and too tentative—for her liking. "But I didn't want to rush you."

She smiled. "You don't have to worry about rushing me. I'm not the little sister of your best friend anymore. I'm a woman. So, you can stop treating me with kid gloves. I know what I want and how I want it."

Trent gazed down at her with those beautiful blue eyes of his for a long moment then he tightened his fingers in her hair and tugged her closer. This time, when his mouth came down on hers, there was no hesitation—and no teasing. This time, he kissed her like he meant it.

She was so wrapped up in the sensation, she barely noticed when he reached down to grab her hips until he picked her up and yanked her onto his lap. The move left her sitting astride his waist, her panty-covered crotch inches above his jean-covered cock. And he'd done it all without breaking the kiss. She would have been impressed, but she was too busy getting aroused to give it much thought.

She wiggled forward until she made firm contact with the bulge in his jeans then draped both arms around his shoulders and focused a hundred percent on kissing the heck out of the hunky Navy SEAL she was lucky enough to have back in her life.

She almost smiled—which was hard to do while kissing—when Trent's hands slipped around her waist and settled on her butt. Considering the way he'd squeezed and caressed that part of her body last night when they'd been making out on this very couch, she got the feeling he had a serious thing for her ass.

That was cool with her. She liked the idea of a guy paying attention to her behind. It was one of her favorite places to be touched. She pushed her bottom back against his hands to let him know she was fine with it, and was rewarded with a firm massage that made her gasp out loud.

Unable to control herself any more, she

yanked at the hem of his T-shirt, intending to drag it over his head. Unfortunately, that was a little difficult to do while they were still engaged in their kiss. She had no choice but to pull away, which made Trent groan in complaint. But while he might be unhappy about her breaking the kiss, it didn't keep him from helping her get his shirt over his head. Between the two of them, they got the thing off and whipped it across the room. Then she sat back on his thighs and enjoyed the view of the most amazing collection of muscles she'd ever seen in her life. Well-rounded shoulders, thick pecs and biceps, rippling abs. It was enough to make a woman cry with joy. She slowly reached out until the palms of her hands came in contact with the warm muscles of his chest. His heart beat under her fingers, the steady rhythm and the rise and fall of his chest almost hypnotizing her.

"You're overdressed," he murmured.

Sliding his hands underneath her top, he quickly stripped it off and tossed it aside. Holding her captive with his gaze, he reached behind her and slowly undid the clasp on her bra. As she slid the straps down her arms and shrugged out of it, his eyes moved lower to catch the reveal. The hungry way he looked at her bare breasts made heat pool between her legs. She had to admit, she really liked having him look at her that way.

Trent leaned forward, his strong arms enveloping her and pulling her close as he pressed his mouth to her neck and began kissing and nibbling a fiery path straight down to her breasts. Lyla arched her back, offering them up to him, moaning long and low as his lips traced a line back and forth from one nipple to the other, teasing, biting, and kissing them until she thought she would go insane.

That was when he got really serious, running his tongue around and around each nipple until they stiffened into hard, tender peaks. Then he drew them into his mouth and suckled them, lavishing them with so much attention she had to wonder if nipple orgasms were a real thing.

Lyla wrapped her arms around him, weaving her fingers in his hair as she closed her eyes and gave herself over to the pleasurable sensations.

But after a while—she wasn't sure how long—she started feeling guilty for simply sitting on his lap, doing nothing. Maybe it was time she returned the favor. With an impressive show of willpower, if she did say so herself, she tightened her grip in his hair and pulled him away from her breasts. Urging his head back until his face was turned up to hers, she touched her lips to his for a quick kiss.

"My turn," she whispered softly before sliding off his lap and dropping to her knees in front of him.

She'd be lying if she said she didn't like the way his eyes widened at seeing her in that position.

Lyla placed her hands on the insides of his jean-covered thighs, shoving his knees wider so she could scoot forward. His muscles tensed and flexed beneath her fingers as she got closer to his erection. She was fairly certain his breathing quickened a little, too.

When she reached her goal, she immediately got to work on the buckles, snaps, and zippers standing in the way of what she was after. Trent helped, shifting his weight on the couch as necessary to let her drag his jeans over his hips and down his legs. It took a bit longer to get him the rest of the way undressed, thanks to the biker boots he wore. But, soon enough, she had him standing in front of her wearing nothing but a pair of boxer briefs that were screaming under the strain of trying to contain his hard cock.

Trent's lower body was just as perfect as the rest of him. As she'd suspected, he didn't have the thick, bulging muscles of a bodybuilder. He was leaner and more ripped than that. As she sat back and took him all in, appreciating how perfect he was, an unexpected realization dawned on her. If she'd thought kneeling in front of him while he was sitting on the couch was nice, kneeling in front of him while he was standing was even better. She'd certainly never been the submissive type, but this position was seriously working for her.

She looked up at him with a smile. "That underwear looks a little uncomfortable. Maybe I should help you get it off."

She didn't wait for a reply, though the sexy grin on his face offered a good clue he was all for anything she had in mind. Wiggling forward on her knees a little, she slipped her fingers into the waistband of his boxer briefs, letting the anticipation build as she slowly exposed his hard cock then shoved his underwear down his thighs.

Lyla stared. Damn, he looked good enough to eat. Which was appropriate since that was what she had in mind.

Licking her lips, she wrapped her fingers around his thick shaft, moaning at how hard he was. Getting a better grip around him, she tugged him forward and dipped her head to take him into her mouth. The chuckle he let out quickly turned into a groan of pleasure as she swirled her tongue around the head of his cock, moving her hand up and down at the same time. Mmm, he tasted delicious.

She'd planned to take her time teasing him and making a game of it, but now that she had him in her mouth, that plan got tossed out the window. She couldn't help it. The urge to make him come took over, and she began moving faster and faster.

She took him deeper then, loving the sensation as the tip of his shaft touched the back of her throat. In between, she caressed him with her hand, making sure she paid attention to all his sensitive spots. And he wasn't shy about letting her know exactly where those were.

But just when Lyla was sure he was close, when the taste of him on her tongue convinced her he was about to orgasm, Trent reached down, hauled her away from his cock and tugged her to her feet.

"Hey, I was working down there," she complained.

"Condoms," he said urgently. "Please tell me you have some."

She was tempted to say she didn't, just to get back at him for interrupting what she'd been doing. But she couldn't. She was too crazy aroused to do something so childish. If he was eager to move on to any activity requiring a condom, she wasn't going to stop him.

"Yes," she said, nudging him back until he had no choice but to sit that sexy butt of his down on the couch. "But I want you to stay right here while I get them. I mean it. Don't even think about moving."

He stayed where he was, looking so damn sexy wearing nothing but a smile and a hard-on. "I wouldn't dream of going anywhere. Unless you take too long, in which case I'm coming to look for you. And take you in whatever position and location I happen to find you."

Lyla suddenly had a vision of Trent taking her from behind as she dug around in her medicine cabinet for the box of condoms she kept there. That visual was more than a little thrilling.

"I may just have to think about that," she murmured before turning and heading for her bathroom.

As she walked slowly away, she unzipped her skirt and slowly shimmied it over her hips, forcing her panties down at the same time.

With a few kicks and wiggles, she had her skirt, and panties off and shoved across the floor before she reached the hallway leading away from the living room. Then she threw a glance over her shoulder, just to see if he was checking out her bottom. He was gazing at her derriere like it was the yummiest dish on an all-you-can-eat buffet.

Oh, yeah. He definitely had a thing for her bottom.

Lyla maintained her poise, walking away slowly and sexily—at least until she was out of sight. Then she took off running at top speed, almost busting her butt when her feet nearly slid out from under as she turned into the bathroom. She quickly rifled through her medicine cabinet until she found what she was looking for. She opened the box to pull one out then changed her mind. Something told her she might need more than one condom before this evening was done.

She ran into the living room, sliding to a stop in front of him, dignity tossed aside as her excitement took over.

Trent started to get up, but she stopped him with a look as she yanked a condom out of the box and dropped to her knees in front of him.

"Remember what I said about not moving?"

she murmured as she tore the foil package open and started getting Trent's hard shaft all wrapped up for the ride. "Nothing has changed. I want you right where you are."

He didn't say a word as she finished getting the condom rolled down then climbed onto his lap. Lyla got his cock positioned exactly where she wanted then slowly began to move up and down, taking him in a little bit at a time even though she was wetter than she could ever remember being. Not that she was in a rush. Now that she was on top of him, she decided she could happily spend the whole night there.

Trent gazed into her eyes as he casually rested his hands on her hips. Not trying to speed her up, but simply guiding her a bit deeper with every trip down his shaft. When she finally sat all the way down, he was so deep inside her all she could do was sit there gasping and looking back into those blue eyes of his.

"Do you know how beautiful you are?" he whispered, his face so close to hers she could feel his warm breath bathing her skin.

Lyla was so entranced with the way he was looking at her, not to mention how amazing he felt inside her, she'd almost completely missed what he'd said. Then it sank in, and she blushed, not only from the words, but the way he'd said it. No one had ever looked at her the way Trent was right now.

"No, I can't say that I do." She looped her arms around his shoulders then leaned in to kiss him. "But I don't think I could get tired of hearing you say it."

They sat there like that for a long time, exploring each other's mouths while he was still nestled inside her. Then, almost of its own accord, her body began undulating up and down.

Trent let her ride him like that for a while, but he must have grown impatient because his grip on her hips tightened and he urged her up and down on his cock more forcefully.

Her sighs turned to moans as he pounded into her harder, making her clit tingle and her whole body spasm. She was going to come soon; she could feel it. Then Trent shifted his hands from her hip to cup her ass, pumping his hips in time with her movements.

Lyla buried her face in Trent's neck, holding on for dear life as he thrust into her so hard she thought she might explode. All at once, the tingles that had been steadily building inside her exploded, and she came so hard she was sure she would pass out.

But she didn't. Instead she continued to orgasm, the waves of pleasure building and cresting over and over as Trent continued to pound into her like he'd never stop. He squeezed her ass tighter, letting out a hoarse groan as he came with her.

When Trent was finally done making her come—and she fully accepted it was his decision to allow her to stop—she clung to him.

"You've ruined me," she panted against the warm skin of his shoulder, fighting to catch her breath as her body continue to spasm around him. "I'll never come that hard again in my life. That was the best it's ever going to get."

Trent chuckled, not even out of breath. "Grab that box of condoms, and let's go see if I can prove you wrong."

Lyla did as he ordered, her body running on auto pilot more than anything else. There was no way they could make love again so soon. It simply didn't work like that.

But as Trent wrapped her legs around his waist, then got a firm grip on her butt and effortlessly stood up, she wondered if she was wrong. If the hard cock inside her was any indication, Trent wasn't done with her yet.

CHAPTER
Seven

"S O, TRENT, ARE YOU STAYING WITH YOUR PARENTS while you're home on leave?"

The casual way Lyla's mother asked the question was totally ruined by her knowing expression as she eyed Lyla and Trent sitting side by side on the couch. Her mom knew there was something going on between them, though how the hell she'd figured out they were sleeping together was beyond Lyla. She and Trent had only set foot in her parents' house five minutes ago.

"Actually, I'm staying in Lyla's guest room," Trent said. "She thought it would be a good way for me to save a little money and not as stressful as staying at my parents' ranch."

Thankfully, Trent was smart enough not to lie outright to her mother, Lyla thought. Pilar Torres would have seen through the fib in a second.

From where he sat in his favorite chair,

Lyla's father lifted his brow so high she thought he might pull a muscle. Her mother, on the other hand, didn't bat an eye. More evidence that she knew Lyla was getting busy with her very own Texas SEAL.

"That's very nice of you, Lyla." Her mom sipped her iced tea. "I'm sure you two are having fun catching up on old times."

Lyla stifled a groan. Yeah, her mom knew, without a doubt. She was probably already envisioning a house full of chubby-cheeked grandkids in the near future. In some ways, her mother was exactly like Trent's. They both wanted their children to settle down and start a family. But there was one difference. Trent had plenty of other brothers and sisters who'd done their jobs and provided handfuls of squirming bundles of joy. Trent had been given a little grace time when it came to adding to the clan. Lyla's parents had only her and Marco, and it was looking more and more like her brother never was going to hold up his end of the obligation. That put all the burden on Lyla. Right now, her mother was smiling like a woman who'd won first prize for her churros at the county fair. Lyla had to admit she might be partly responsible for that. After the night she and Trent had shared, she couldn't keep the silly grin off her face.

She and Trent had intended to come over here to talk to her parents about Marco much earlier, but they hadn't finished making love until almost sunrise and ended up sleeping until almost noon. Lyla wasn't complaining about the lack of sleep. If she could have as much fun every night as she'd had last night, she'd give up sleeping completely.

When they'd finally collapsed into each other's arms as the sun was peeking over the horizon, she'd arrived at the conclusion that every time with him was going to be amazing. He was an orgasm whisperer.

But as wonderful as last night had been, this morning had been even more perfect. They'd lain in bed naked, eating breakfast burritos and planning out their vacation to Disney World on her laptop. Of course, after last night, she wasn't sure how often they'd leave their resort. As fun as all the rides in the parks were sure to be, she couldn't help but think she'd found her favorite ride already.

"Lyla, are you listening to me?" Her father's deep voice jerked her out of her reverie.

"Sorry," she said. "What?"

"I asked when you saw that rotten, no-good brother of yours last."

The proud owner of a landscaping company, her father had a few more lines on his tanned face than when he'd started the business and could have a brusque way about him sometimes, but he had a soft spot when it came to her and her mother. Her brother? Not so much.

"Miguel," her mother rebuked softly, almost reluctantly. "Don't talk about Marco like that. He's trying. He has a decent job now."

Lyla had to force herself not to plant her face in the palms of her hands to escape the embarrassment of what was coming. This was why she'd put off telling her parents what a mess her idiot brother had made of his life.

"Trying?" Her father snorted. "Are you kidding me? That boy of ours is a dirtbag. He's been a dirtbag since he was a teenager, and he'll always be a dirtbag." He pinned Lyla with a stern look. "And if you're not careful, he's going to take you down with him."

"That's not true!" The glance Lyla's mother gave her was almost desperate, like she needed someone other than herself to believe it. "Marco loves his sister, Miguel. He'd never do anything to hurt her."

Lyla winced. No, Marco would never be violent with her physically. But the way he was throwing his life away hurt all the same.

"Oh, please! That kid has never done a single thing for anyone but himself," her dad insisted. "And he doesn't care who gets hurt in the process."

Lyla sighed. Her mother looked angry and probably would have gotten into an argument with her husband if Trent hadn't been there. She looked around at the living room reminiscent of an old-style Spanish hacienda, taking in the warm earth tones of the stucco walls and exposed dark wood beams on the high ceiling, mentally counting to ten. It was stupid coming here to tell them about Marco. It was only going to make things worse.

It had been like this since Marco began using drugs in high school. Her mom and dad had been furious and disappointed in him, but had both tried to help him get clean. Unfortunately, nothing they tried worked for long. While her mother still prayed he'd get his life together, her father had washed his hands of the whole mess. The way he saw it, Lyla and her mother were enabling Marco. After what had happened the past few days, she couldn't say he was wrong.

Across the room, her father regarded her thoughtfully. "It looks like you have something on your mind, Lyla. If you have something to say about Marco, spit it out."

She hesitated, tempted to lie, but what good would that do? Her parents had a right to know Marco was involved with the same people who'd gotten him sent to jail before. Better they hear it from her than from the police.

Beside her, Trent reached over and took her hand, giving it a squeeze. She offered him a small smile then took a deep breath and launched into the whole story. She left out the part about the fight Trent had gotten into with Cobb's goons, and glossed over the fact Marco had a woman in his life now. Other than that, she gave it to them straight.

They took it the way she'd thought they would. Her father cursed, and her mother cried. Seeing them both hurting made tears sting Lyla's eyes, and she blinked them back angrily. She could smack Marco for what he was doing to their family.

Lyla and Trent commiserated with them about Marco for a little while longer before she told her parents they should get going.

"Aren't you staying for dinner?" her mom asked. "We're having chicken tostadas."

Lyla hadn't really thought about it. Her mother was a fantastic cook, though, so she certainly wouldn't mind. She gave Trent a questioning look.

"Sounds good to me," he said.

Her mother beamed. "Good. It will give us a chance to catch up with Trent and talk about something other than your brother."

Lyla was all for that. "I'll give you a hand."

Her mom had already mixed the shredded chicken with lime juice and the requisite spices, as well as prepared the homemade refried beans, so all they had to do was assemble the tostadas.

"Okay," her mother said as they spread the beans over the batch of crispy fried tortillas she had made. "What didn't you tell us about Marco out in the living room? I know there has to be something more to it."

Lyla sighed. Her mom had always been good at knowing when she was hiding something.

"Marco's been seeing Dana, the woman who owns the gallery where he shows his sculptures," she said.

Her mother stopped what she was doing, the spoon in her hand hovering over the bowl of refried beans, her dark eyes lighting up. "He has? That's wonderful!"

Lyla scowled. "Yeah, well, I think he just sabotaged the relationship. Not that it matters because he's probably going to end up in prison again." Lyla dumped a spoonful of beans on another tortilla. "Dad's right. Marco *is* too stupid to know when he has a good thing going."

"Maybe it's not what you think." Her mother scooped out more beans. "Maybe Marco isn't involved in that life anymore."

"Mom, Trent and I were right there when Marco walked in with Cobb. They were down in Mexico together. What else would he be doing but something involving drugs?"

Her mother closed her eyes for a moment then opened them. "What that boy needs is someone to talk some sense into him and get him to see he's throwing his life away."

Lyla reached for a handful of shredded Monterey Jack cheese and sprinkled it on top of the beans. "Yeah, well, I don't think he'll listen to Dad."

Or Trent, for that matter. She hated to even ask him. He'd already done so much by coming out here with her to look for Marco.

"I'm not talking about your father, dear. I mean you."

Lyla did a double take. "Me?"

"Yes, you." Her mom smiled. "Why do you think you're the one he always turns to when he's in trouble?"

Lyla snorted. "Because he knows I'm the only one dumb enough to keep answering the phone when he calls."

"That's not it, and you know it. Even though he's older than you are, Marco looks up to you," Her mother transferred the tostadas to a baking sheet then put them in the oven to broil. "Don't give up on him, dear. Not when he needs you the most. Please."

Lyla wasn't as confident as her mother about her ability to influence Marco. If she had any pull with him, he wouldn't be working for Cobb right now. But he was still her big brother, and she loved him.

"Okay," she told her mother with a sigh. "I'm not promising he'll listen, but I'll talk to him again."

Her mother sagged with relief. "Thank you."

They fell silent as they moved around the kitchen, Lyla setting the table while her mother got the salsa ready.

"So," her mom said, placing the bowl of homemade salsa on the table. "You and Trent."

Lyla concentrated on putting the cutlery beside each plate, refusing to rise to the bait. "He's just a friend I'm putting up in my guest bedroom while he's in town."

"Uh-huh." Her mother folded her arms and gave her a knowing look. "I know you've always liked him, Lyla."

"Mom, we're just friends."

"Lyla, I've seen you with other men you've dated, and I never saw you look at any of them the way you look at Trent. You're falling for him, aren't you?"

Lyla was about to tell her mother that was crazy. Trent had been in town for a grand total of two days. They hadn't gone on an official date, regardless of the fact they'd slept together. There was no way she could have feelings for him yet. But then she realized that was a lie. As insane as it seemed, she was starting to fall for him.

"Would that be so bad?" she finally asked, turning to face her mother. "Yeah, it would be crazy trying to have a long distance relationship with a guy out in San Diego while I'm in Texas, but aren't you the one always saying a woman should go where her heart tells her to go?"

Lyla's mother rested gentle hands on her shoulders, her expression soft. "Yes. And if you feel that way about Trent, I'm all for it. But, honey, he's a SEAL. Are you seriously ready to get involved with a Navy guy?"

Lyla laughed. "You make it sound like he's an alien from another planet. I know he's a SEAL. We've had that conversation."

Her mother's brow furrowed. "Was it a real conversation, or was it like the ones your father and I have about Marco where we both say a lot stuff but don't really communicate?"

"What are you trying to say?"

"Lyla, honey, Navy SEALs do a lot of dangerous stuff. Emphasis on *a lot*," her mother said. "His parents have told me he's usually deployed eight months out of the year with no way to contact him. And when he isn't, he's off God knows where training. There's not a second of his life when he's not on duty. Even now, while he's on leave, he could get a call and be on a plane to go someplace neither one of us has probably ever heard of in an hour. That's what it means to be a SEAL. Is that something you're ready to be part of?"

Lyla didn't answer. While she and Trent had talked about his job, they hadn't done more than scratch the surface. But heck, they'd just started seeing each other.

"Mom, I like Trent, and I'm pretty sure he feels the same about me," she finally said. "But that's as far as we've gotten. Maybe it will turn into something else, but right now, I'm okay with where we are."

Her mother gave her a small smile. "I'm okay with that, too, Lyla. I simply want to make sure you and Trent have a serious conversation about what you'll be getting yourself into if you want to make a commitment to him. I want you going into this with your eyes wide open."

Lyla nodded. "I am, Mom."

"Good."

Lyla chewed on her lower lip as her mother walked over to get the tostadas out of the oven. The truth was, she'd been so giddy about reconnecting with Trent she hadn't thought too much about what a future with him would look like. She enjoyed being with him, and the sex was off the charts, so she'd definitely like to keep seeing him. Yeah, it would be hard doing the long-distance thing, but the truth was, that wasn't the worst part of the deal.

Trent being deployed for months on end without her knowing where he was, doing all kinds of dangerous crap, was the part that really made her hesitate. Lyla wasn't sure she was the kind of woman who could handle that.

Maybe her mother was right. Maybe it was time she and Trent had a serious conversation, before she let herself fall any further for him.

CHAPTER
Eight

Y OU WERE QUIET ON THE WAY HOME. EVERYTHING okay?" Trent asked, closing the door of her apartment behind them and pulling her into his arms.

He'd known something was bothering Lyla the moment they'd sat down to dinner with her parents. His gut told him it had something to do with whatever she and her mother had talked about while making the tostadas. He'd thought at first it had to do with Marco, though that didn't seem right. But if not that, then what?

Lyla melted against his chest, resting her cheek on his shoulder and wrapping her arms around him so tightly his ribs creaked. Not that he was complaining. He liked being in her arms more than he ever could have imagined.

"Mom told me some stuff tonight that made me realize there are a lot of things about you I don't know," she said softly.

He pulled away to study her face. "What kind of things?"

She lifted her head, her eyes bright with unshed tears. His gut tightened. If he didn't know any better, he'd think she was about to break up with him. That should be impossible since they hadn't been together long enough to actually break up.

"How dangerous is your job?" she asked.

To say the question caught him off guard was an understatement. He definitely hadn't seen that coming. But that explained her expression. He'd seen variations of it on other women he'd dated. Usually before everything went to crap.

"Come on," he said. "Let's sit down."

Holding onto her hand, he led her over to the couch then took a seat beside her. The trepidation in her eyes made his chest hurt.

"Lyla, you already know that SEALs do a dangerous job. We talked about that. Where's this coming from?"

She bit her lip, as if trying to figure out what she wanted to say. "My mom told me you do a lot of *really* dangerous stuff, and that you're gone eight months out of the year. Is that true?"

It took a moment for Lyla's words to sink in. If the two of them had just been messing around and having a good time while he was in town on leave then how dangerous his job was, or how often he was deployed, shouldn't have been an issue for her. But it obviously was, and that made him think she was starting to develop feelings for him. Maybe even the same kind he was beginning to feel for her.

"Yeah. In general, it's true," he said, choosing his words carefully. "My Team and I go to craphole places all around the world and do things that should probably be impossible. But that's what I'm trained to do, and I do it well. SEALs get the job done, but more than that, we cover each other's backs while we're doing it. We have a simple mantra on my Team— *Everyone Comes Home*. And we'll do anything necessary to make sure everyone does."

She considered that for a moment then nodded. "Okay. What about the deployments? Are you gone that long?"

He wished he could sugarcoat it and tell her it wasn't that bad. But sometimes it was, and she deserved to know that.

"It can be," he said gently. "Sometimes I'm gone for three months at a time. I've been gone as long as seven months but as short as a week. It's whatever the mission calls for. Now, I will tell you the other single guys and I volunteer for extra missions to give the guys with wives and girlfriends more time at home."

A glimmer of something—hope, he supposed—showed in her eyes. "So, in theory, you wouldn't always be gone that long?"

Trent winced. He knew what she wanted to hear, what she *needed* to hear. That being with a SEAL wouldn't be that bad. But as much as he might want to keep seeing Lyla, it would be wrong to mislead her.

"It could be less," he admitted. "But if you're considering whether you want to get involved with me, then you need to face the very real possibility that there will almost certainly be long stretches when I'm not there with you. Worse, there are going to be times when you have no idea where I am or when I'm coming back."

And with those words, any possibility of a future with Lyla had just gone out the frigging window. He could see it in her eyes. He was stunned at how crappy that made him feel, considering the short amount of time they'd been together. She'd clearly gotten under his skin a lot deeper than he'd imagined.

"What kind of woman could deal with that?" she wondered.

"Not many." He offered her a sad smile. "Which is probably why so few of the guys on my Team are in a serious relationship with anyone."

Lyla considered that. "But some SEALs get married, right? Or at least get into steady relationships?"

"Sure," he said. "My former chief has been married for over twenty years, and two of the other guys currently on the Team—Chasen and Logan—recently met women they think are in it for the long haul. But I know it's tough on all of them, and I can't blame you for not wanting to get involved with a SEAL. It's probably better we figure it out now, before either one of us gets hurt."

Lyla blinked. "Wait. What? I'm not saying I don't want to try!"

Trent stared at her. Okay, now he was confused. "But you just said you weren't sure what kind of woman could deal with that life. Asking you to consider putting yourself through something like that is more than I have a right to do, regardless of how I feel about you."

She leaned forward. "Were you asking?"

Crap. His head was spinning so fast, he was practically dizzy. "Asking what?"

"Were you asking me to put myself through that...with you?" she clarified.

He opened his mouth then closed it again.

He needed a lifeline in the worst frigging way. "I thought that's what this conversation was about. Whether you wanted to get involved with me beyond these two weeks of leave."

"Is that what you want?" she asked.

Trent felt like he was standing naked in a minefield with no idea which direction to go. All he knew for sure was that the next step he took was going to be extremely meaningful to the continuation of his existence.

"Well...yeah. I thought that was obvious." When Lyla's eyes widened, he quickly held up his hands. "But that was before."

"Before what?" she asked, frowning in blatant confusion.

Welcome to the frigging club.

"Before you made it clear that you're not interested in getting involved with a SEAL."

She sat back, her frown replaced with a look of hurt. "I never said that."

He should just give up now because he was so out of his depth here it wasn't funny. He'd dealt with countless life and death situations as a SEAL, from ambushes to malfunctioning equipment to people with guns threatening to kill him in languages he sometimes didn't understand, but he'd never felt this overwhelmed.

Finally, he took a deep breath and decided

to approach it from a different direction.

"Maybe we need to start over," he suggested.

Lyla nodded but didn't say anything.

Okay. It looked like he was going to have to start. "I know this thing between us is happening fast, and maybe it's just me, but I think we really click."

Lyla was silent, like she was waiting for more.

"If I was being smart about this, I'd wait to say anything until after we see how things go on our vacation," he continued. "But I've already decided I don't need that much time to figure out something this obvious." He ran his hand through his hair. "This is going to sound insane, but I haven't felt this way about anyone in a really long time. Okay, that's not true. Actually, I've never felt this way about a woman. I don't know. Maybe it's because we've known each other since we were kids, but there's this crazy connection between us, and I'd really like to see where it goes."

Lyla opened her mouth to say something, but he charged on. Damn the torpedoes and all that.

"I know the idea of getting involved with a man in my line of work probably scares the hell out of you, and I'm not trying to downplay how tough it's going to be. All I'm asking is a chance to see if maybe we can make it work. If you're interested, I mean." He shrugged. "If you're not and have no interest in trying, I completely understand."

Trent held his breath, waiting. Damn, it felt good getting all this stuff off his chest. Even if he hadn't known it was there.

One moment Lyla was sitting there, studying him like he was a curious exhibit at the petting zoo, and the next she was leaning forward to kiss him. He was caught completely off guard, but luckily kissing was an involuntary reaction—for him, at least—so his mouth did its thing without much guidance from his head.

He was just about to slide his fingers into her hair when she pulled back and regarded him with soft doe eyes that made his heart melt.

"Yes, I'm terrified at the idea of getting involved with a man who's going to disappear for months at a time to dangerous places I've most likely never heard of." She reached up to caress his scruffy jaw. "But as scared as I am about all that, I'm more scared about walking away from something that could be special without giving it a shot."

Trent almost sagged with relief. He kissed

her again, this time with his head fully engaged. "Does that mean we're going to try our hands at that long-distance thing?"

Lyla stood up and moved over to sit on his lap. "Yeah, I guess that's exactly what it means," she said, looping her arms around his neck. "I've never done the long-distance thing before, but if I can handle that, hopefully, I can handle everything else that comes with being with a SEAL."

He glided his hand down her back, resting it on the curve of her bottom. "There will be times when things get rough."

She nodded. "I know. But you said something a couple days ago about not worrying about what might be, and instead focusing on what's in front of you. That's what I'm going to do, and let the other stuff take care of itself."

He touched his forehead to hers. "And while the other stuff is taking care of itself, we'll worry about taking care of each other."

"That sounds like a good plan." She tilted her head up to kiss him, slipping her tongue into his mouth to tease and tangle with his.

He groaned as she ground on his lap. Well, on his erection, actually.

"He woke up fast, didn't he?" she laughed, slowly grinding her perfect ass against his hard-on. "Maybe we should take this into the bedroom."

He grinned. "My thoughts exactly."

Trent got to his feet, cradling Lyla in his arms and heading that way. The moment he set her down on the floor, she kicked off her shoes and peeled off her dress while he went to work on his T-shirt and jeans. She won the let's-see-who-can-get-naked-first race. The view of her ass as she wiggled across the bed to grab a condom from the nightstand was so awesome, he had to slow down and appreciate it. He quickly stripped off the rest of his clothes once she flipped back over and beckoned him onto the bed, however.

The urge to pounce on her was unreal, but he controlled himself, slowing down enough to reach out and drag her toward him. When he had her bottom positioned right at the edge of the bed, he shoved her legs wide and dropped to his knees in front of her. Spreading her legs wide, he leaned forward and pressed his lips to the delectable skin of her inner thigh. Damn, she tasted good.

He nibbled his way down one inner thigh and up the other, avoiding the junction between them for the moment as he went back and forth, enjoying teasing her a little and knowing the anticipation would turn her on even more.

Lyla weaved her fingers in his hair, trying to steer him exactly where she wanted him. He refused to concede control, though. Only when she was squirming on the bed did he finally relent and press his mouth on her pussy.

"Yes," she breathed.

He slowly traced his tongue up and down her folds and around her clit, groaning in appreciation, entranced with the beautiful view of her getting more and more excited by the second.

"Right there," she said as he focused solely on her clit. "Just. Like. That."

Trent held on tightly as she orgasmed against his mouth, her thighs and abs tensing and spasming as waves of pleasure rolled through her. He glanced up to see her cover her mouth with her hand as if trying to muffle her scream. It worked for a while, but finally the wave must have crested too high because she let it out, her cries bouncing off the walls.

He'd never heard anything more beautiful in his life.

When he'd wrung as much pleasure from her as he could, he gently moved his mouth away from her clit, turning his head to the side to kiss her inner thigh again. Lyla lay gasping, and Trent let her, enjoying the sighs she made as the post-orgasm tremors continued to ripple through her body.

When her breathing was once again close to normal, he stood up and searched the bed until he found the condom she'd tossed aside earlier. He got himself all wrapped and climbed onto the bed as Lyla opened her eyes.

"Hey there," she said dreamily.

He settled slowly between her legs, keeping most of his weight on his knees and elbows as he smiled down at her. "Hey yourself."

He shifted his hips until the head of his shaft was lodged at her very wet opening. They were so perfect for each other, there wasn't any of the normal fumbling that usually occurred when two people started sleeping together. They fit together like two pieces of a puzzle.

Lyla's legs came up to wrap around his waist as he slid in deep. Her heels urged him to go deeper and faster, but he took his time. This felt too good to rush a second of it.

Trent held himself above her, gazing at her as he went as deep as he could go. He moved slowly, thrusting gently, loving the way her eyes widened a little each time he buried his length fully inside her.

Her legs tightening around him, Lyla clutched his shoulders and pulled him down, her nails digging in as she got closer to orgasm. He kept his movements slow and deliberate, letting the pleasure build for both of them. When he felt his climax start, it was his turn to bury his face in her neck.

It had never felt this good with a woman. This right.

He held off until he felt her tremble under him then he let himself go, coming with her as she cried out. He came so hard he made himself dizzy, but he didn't slow his thrusts. He wanted more than anything for this to be the most perfect moment she'd ever had.

Lyla stirred feelings he'd never felt before. It seemed insane to fall this fast for someone, and the guys on the Team would almost certainly tell him he was crazy, but he knew better. When something was right, it was right.

Lifting his head, he gazed down at her. "You're so beautiful, it takes my breath away to look at you. It makes me wonder how the hell I ever got lucky enough to have you stumble back into my life."

She reached up, tugging him down for a kiss. "Maybe luck had nothing to do with it," she murmured against his mouth. "Sometimes

God takes a hand in our lives, and miracles happen."

"To miracles, then," he said softly.

"To miracles," she whispered, kissing him again.

CHAPTER
Nine

LYLA COULDN'T RESIST GLANCING OVER HER SHOULDER as she walked across the gravel parking lot in front of the big warehouse. She should have taken Trent up on his offer to come with her to see her brother. Even in the daytime, this part of town was deserted. Why the heck did her brother have his studio in the industrial area?

She hurried the last half dozen steps leading to the central walkway that would take her there. This was probably going to be a complete waste of time. Her brother might be back in Mexico already. She should have gone to Trent's parents with him instead of meeting him there later. But she thought her brother would be more likely to listen if she talked to him alone.

After dropping Trent off at the ranch, she'd driven to Marco's apartment, and when he hadn't been there, she'd come to his art studio. She still wasn't quite sure what she was going to say to get him to stop this insanity before it was too late. She supposed she'd start by reminding him that if he got caught on a deal-related charge for a third time, he'd likely go to prison for life. If that didn't work, she'd try to get him to see what he was throwing away with Dana and all he'd accomplished as an artist.

She'd just about reached his studio when approaching footsteps made her jump. Her heart kicked into high gear as two men appeared out of the shadows between the buildings and came toward her. One of them was the guy Trent had gotten into a fight with and head-butted at Cobb's club. There was a big bandage across his broken nose and dark bruising around both eyes. The jerk must have been there to see Marco. And she doubted it had anything to do with looking at his artwork. She supposed that answered her question about whether Marco was in his studio or not.

Lyla was torn for a moment between turning and heading back to her car or continuing to her brother's. Telling herself they wouldn't try anything in broad daylight, she ignored the sleazy looks they sent her way and hurried past them to Marco's. When she got there, she quickly shoved open the heavy metal door.

"Marco!" she shouted.

Her voice echoed around her as she walked through the smaller room he used as an office and straight into the big open work space filled with racks of sheet metal and various thicknesses of pipes and rods, overhead cranes, welders, and sanding and grinding equipment. As she went, she couldn't help noticing the three new sculpture pieces her brother was in the process of making. From the haze of smoke and the acrid stench of superheated metal hanging in the air, she knew Marco had to be there somewhere.

She was about to call out again when she caught sight of a foot and part of a leg sticking out from behind a big workbench. Her heart plummeted.

"Marco!"

He sat up as she ran over. Her eyes widened at the sight of the fresh bruise on his jaw and the blood trickling down his chin from a split lip.

She dropped to the floor beside him, reaching out to check him for other injuries. "What happened?"

That was a stupid question. It was obvious what had happened to her brother. Cobb had been sending some kind of message and used his muscle-headed goons to deliver it.

"I'm fine," Marco said, waving her hands away as she tried to see if he was bleeding anywhere else. "It was just a misunderstanding."

She shook her head, knowing that was crap. "Like hell." She dug her phone out of her purse. "I saw Cobb's men outside. They beat you up. I don't know why, and I don't care. But I'm sure as heck not putting up with it. I'm calling the police."

"You can't do that," Marco said.

"Watch me," she retorted.

She started dialing 9-1-1, but her brother reached out and pulled the phone out of her hand. "Lyla, I'm serious. You can't call the cops, or someone important to me is going to die."

She thought he was simply being dramatic, but the tone of his voice, not to mention the haunted look on his face struck her. Crap. He wasn't kidding.

Lyla sat back on her heels. "Marco, what the hell have you gotten yourself into? I thought you were working for Cobb. Why would he send his men to beat you up?"

He didn't look at her as she dropped her phone back into her purse. "This isn't anything you need to be involved in. Just go home and forget about me. I've made a mess out of my life. I don't want to do the same to yours."

She made a sound of frustration, the urge to choke the crap out of him nearly impossible to resist. What the hell was wrong with him? Had all the drugs he'd done made him stupid?

"You're going to tell me what the hell is going on, or I'm going to walk right out of here right now and call the police," she told him. "You can talk to me, or you can talk to the cops who come here to arrest you. But, one way or the other, you're going to talk."

Her brother scowled. "Okay, I'll tell you. Then you need to go before Cobb thinks you know something that will upset his plans."

Well, that sounded ominous as hell. "What the heck does that mean?"

Marco ignored the question, climbing to his feet then helping her up before walking over to the workbench to pick up a filthy rag to wipe at the blood on his chin. She wanted to tell her brother to use a clean cloth instead, but she didn't bother. He wouldn't listen. He never did.

"That second stint I did at McConnell for possession?" he said, not looking in her direction. "That wasn't my stuff. I agreed to take the hit so Tim wouldn't go down for it. He was looking at his third strike, and he would have been looking at a life sentence."

Lyla stared at him, not sure what the heck

that meant. Okay, that wasn't quite true. She got the gist of it. The drugs the police had found on him that had sent him to jail for another eighteen months hadn't been his but had instead belonged to Tim, whom he'd been arrested with at the time. Her brother had purposely destroyed his life for the piece of crap who'd gotten him sent to prison the first time. All to save Tim from serving a life time sentence.

"Why the hell would you do that?" she demanded. "Why would you go to jail for that a-hole?"

He glanced at her. "When I was in prison for that first nickel, I would have died twenty times over if it wasn't for Tim. He kept me alive in there. I owed him a debt. When it looked like he was going to go down again, I stepped up for him."

Lyla shook her head. He was talking about a world so far outside her understanding, it might as well have been an alien planet.

She pointed at the bloody rag in his hand. "What does any of this have to do with the here and now? You repaid your debt to Tim. Why are you letting them pull you back in?"

"It's complicated."

"So, make it uncomplicated. Before I call the police."

He was silent for so long, she thought he might call her bluff. She wasn't really sure what she'd do if he did.

"Tim wasn't there to cover my back the second time, but he didn't leave me on my own," Marco said softly. "He went to Mr. Cobb and asked for a favor—protection for me while I did time."

Lyla remembered Dana talking about the argument she'd overheard between Marco and Tim right here in this studio. After what Marco had already told her about repaying his debts, she finally had an idea what all this was about.

"And now you owe Cobb," she finished for him.

He nodded. "About three months ago, Mr. Cobb asked me to modify one of my sculptures to carry drugs. It was one that was going to Mexico City for a show. When it came back, it was loaded with fifty pounds of carfentanil."

Lyla closed her eyes, her heart breaking. Her brother had let Cobb use his art to smuggle drugs. If the cops ever found out, Marco would be the one facing a third strike and a life sentence.

"What's carfentanil?" she asked.

She wasn't sure it really mattered, but for some strange reason she wanted to know what her brother had thrown away his life to smuggle.

"It's a synthetic opioid used on very large animals for surgery. Moose, rhinos, elephants—animals like that," he explained. "It's five thousand times more potent than heroin. Assuming it was pure, I can't imagine what the street value of that much stuff would be."

"You did it that one time, so now he wants you to do it again," she surmised.

Everything made sense now—why Marco had been down in Mexico, why he was working on three mammoth sculptures, why Cobb's goons had come calling. The crime boss wanted more sculptures to carry his drugs, and he wanted them now.

"He wants three new pieces for a major showing in Monterrey, Mexico. They're not close to being done, but I'm supposed to get on a truck with them tomorrow morning for a show in a few days. After a week in Monterrey, these new pieces, plus five others that are already there, will be loaded with more carfentanil and put on a truck for a show in Dallas. The drugs, hundreds of pounds of it, will be pulled out there." Her brother swallowed hard. "I don't have a choice."

She snorted. "Of course not. You owe him,

right? Or is it Tim you still owe? Which one is it? I get confused by all these debts you seem to still owe everyone. You've given these people over five years of your life, and that still doesn't seem to be enough for them."

Marco's face darkened. "I'm not doing this for either of them. I'm doing it for Erika."

Lyla tried to remember if she'd ever heard the name before. "Who the heck is Erika?"

She was surprised when a slight smile cracked her brother's visage. It disappeared just as quickly.

"She's Tim's little girl," he said. "Cobb is holding her hostage down in Monterrey. If I don't do exactly what he wants, he'll hurt the kid. He knows I could never let that happen."

If Lyla had been confused before, she was completely baffled now. This didn't make any sense. "Why would Cobb think threatening Tim's kid would convince you to do anything?" Then a crazy thought struck her. "Crap! Is Erika your daughter?"

"What? God, no," Marco said. "But she's the only one in all this who's worth saving. Her mother died of a drug overdose when Tim was in prison with me the first time. When I got out, it was more than Tim could manage, so I started helping take care of her. She's an angel born into a crappy situation. She's the biggest reason I took the fall for Tim this last time. I didn't want Erika to see her dad go to prison again. Cobb knows I'll do anything to keep her safe."

"Even if it means going to prison for life?"

"Even then."

She sighed. What a mess. "Why haven't you called the police and told them about Cobb keeping Erika prisoner?"

Marco let out a short laugh. "Are you kidding me? Do you think the cops care about people like me? Like Erika? They wouldn't give me the time of day. They'd probably revoke my parole and throw me back in prison, the hell with what happens to Erika." His mouth tightened. "I'm going to do this my way, like I always have."

"You're just going to end up in prison, and Erika still won't be any better off," she pointed out. "Even if you're somehow able to make this all work out, you know Cobb isn't going to let you walk away. He's going to keep using Erika to control you until he gets everything he can out of you. You're going to end up back in prison—or dead."

Marco stiffened. "That's my problem to deal with, isn't it?"

Lyla stared at her brother for a moment, feeling the last few threads binding them together snapping away. She was never going to be able to help him. She never could. The only question left was whether she was going to let him pull her down with him when he crashed and burned. She knew what her mother would say, and she knew what her father would say. Now it was time to figure out what she was going to say.

"Yes, it is your problem," she said softly. "And you'll deal with it the same way you always have. Except this time, you'll do it without me there to bail you out."

Tears stinging her eyes, Lyla turned and headed for the door. It tore her heart out to turn her back on her brother, but she simply couldn't keep watching as he did one stupid thing after another. It was time she realized there was only so much a sister could do for her older brother.

Her vision was so blurry, she didn't see Cobb's big bruisers until they were right in front of her, blocking her route to her car.

"What do you want?" she demanded, too heartbroken to be worried about what they might or might not do.

The man with the broken nose smiled. "Your brother piss you off? That junkie has a habit of not taking things as seriously as he probably should."

Lyla might be mad at her brother, but hearing him called a junkie pissed her off. She was about to tell the jerk in front of her exactly that, but he stepped forward and grabbed her arms, dragging her away from her SUV.

"Mr. Cobb asked us to take you down to Mexico to make sure that moron brother of yours understands that what Mr. Cobb wants, Mr. Cobb gets."

The second man laughed, and she looked over her shoulder to see him standing beside a big, dark sedan, smirking. That was when Lyla realized just how much trouble she was in.

Lyla reacted without thinking, swinging wildly at the guy holding her, her poorly-aimed punch hitting him in his bandaged nose by pure chance. He cried out in pain, letting go of her to reach up and protect his bloody nose.

She twisted away and ran for her car, screaming for help and praying she'd get there in time. She didn't get more than three steps when Broken Nose grabbed her by the hair, yanking her back so hard she flew off her feet.

"Where the hell do you think you're going, you stupid bitch?"

Lyla fought and screamed, but it did no

good. Broken Nose and his equally large friend dragged her to the car and threw her in the back seat. Her head hit the edge of the door on the way in, knocking her so dizzy she could do little more than shove ineffectively at her kidnapper as he climbed in beside her.

Her head throbbed as she tried to jerk the door open on her side of the car, ready to throw herself out of the moving vehicle if necessary, but Broken Nose bounced her forehead off the side window and told her to stop making a fuss.

"Unless you want to ride in the trunk all the way to the airport," he added with a laugh.

Lyla had a hard time hearing the words over the stabbing pain in her head. It was on the tip of her tongue to tell him good luck with that since she didn't have a passport. Then again, Cobb wasn't likely to take her out of the country by a route requiring one.

She would have lost it right there, if it wasn't for one simple fact. Trent knew she'd come to see Marco. He'd figure out what happened to her, and he'd do whatever was necessary to find her. She believed that with every fiber of her being.

Trent sighed with relief when he saw Lyla's car sitting in the darkened parking lot outside Marco's studio. For the first time in hours, he felt like he could breathe again.

When five o'clock had come and gone, he'd started texting Lyla, asking if everything was okay and how things had gone with her brother. When he hadn't gotten anything back from her, he'd called, then called again, and again, but her phone had gone to voice mail every time. His parents had picked up on his concern by then and offered him their truck to check on Lyla. He'd taken them up on the offer, and after a quick call to Lyla's parents to ask for Marco's address, he'd headed for his old friend's apartment. Neither Lyla nor her brother was there, but Marco's neighbor told him Lyla had stopped by there more than three hours ago then left when she couldn't find her brother.

Trent's first instinct had been to head straight to Marco's studio, but then he realized he didn't know where it was. It took him a few seconds to figure out what to do, but then he remembered Lyla had called Dana on his phone, so the number would still be in the recently called list.

Dana had freaked a little when he called and asked for the address to Marco's studio. Trent had been tempted to lie and say everything was fine, but his gut told him things weren't fine, so he'd admitted Lyla had gone to see her brother and now she wasn't answering her phone.

Dana had put him on hold to call Marco but had come back on the line less than a minute later saying Marco wasn't answering his phone either.

"Call the moment you learn anything," she told Trent after she gave him the address. "If you see Marco, tell him I love him and I'm sorry things didn't work out differently."

Trent had said he would.

That was fifteen long, agonizing minutes ago, and it had been tough as hell keeping to the speed limit as he drove over here. But seeing Lyla's SUV made the tension wash away. She and Marco must be having one hell of a talk if she'd been here all this time. Hell, maybe he'd be able to call Dana with some good news after this.

But the second he walked into Marco's studio and found his old friend hard at work with a cutting torch—and Lyla nowhere in sight— Trent's gut clenched all over again.

"Marco!" he shouted, getting the other man's attention over the hissing of the torch. "Where's your sister?"

Marco turned at the sound of his name, staring at Trent through the dark goggles he was wearing. He slowly turned off the cutting torch and tossed it onto a workbench with a careless clatter. The goggles soon followed, revealing fresh bruises and a split lip that was swelling up pretty good. The abuse looked fresh, making Trent wonder if Lyla had taken her anger out on her brother. No way. Regardless of how much of a moron her brother was, Lyla loved him too much to ever lay a hand on him, even if that was probably what the guy needed.

"Where's Lyla?" Trent asked again.

Marco shook his head. "No idea. I haven't seen her."

If Lyla's car out in the parking lot wasn't a dead giveaway, the look crossing Marco's face was. The man was lying his ass off.

All kind of dark scenarios played through Trent's mind right then, most of them involving Marco losing his cool and doing something to his sister. But worse were the thoughts that one of the assholes in her brother's world had finally reached out and affected someone besides Marco himself.

Either way, Trent was in no mood to play around. He closed the distance between him and Marco in three quick steps, yanking his friend off his feet and slamming him back onto the table with the cutting torch and pieces of metal scrap.

"Her car is right outside, Marco, so I know she was here," Trent ground out as he balled his fists into the man's shirt and thumped him down on the table a couple of times. "Now, you're either going to tell me where she is, or I'm going to beat the living shit out of you then turn you over to the police. Maybe I'll tell them I saw you with a load of drugs at Cobb's club. With your background, something tells me they'll believe me."

Marco's eyes widened, as if he'd finally figured out Trent was serious as shit. "You can't do that!"

"I'm pretty sure I can."

Marco shook his head like crazy. "If I get arrested and can't finish these sculptures, Lyla is dead."

Trent's heart pounded so fast he got dizzy. "What the hell are you talking about?"

"Cobb's guys grabbed her over an hour ago. He called and told me," Marco said. "She's probably on a private plane bound for Mexico right now."

Shit.

"And you didn't think about calling the

cops?" Trent shouted. "Didn't think about calling me?"

He could kill Marco. Right now, he had a hard time believing this man used to be his best friend.

"I couldn't," Marco said. "Cobb wants these sculptures on the way down to Monterrey, Mexico tomorrow morning so he can load them with drugs for the return trip. He took Lyla to make sure I do as he wants. If I don't get these pieces to him by tomorrow night, he'll take it out on her."

Trent didn't say anything for a long time, his mind racing as he fought to stay calm. He wanted to pound Marco senseless for dragging Lyla into this, but that wouldn't do any good. If he was right, she was out of the country already and on her way to Mexico.

"Where exactly did those assholes take her?" he demanded.

Marco shook his head. "This isn't anything you can get involved in. Cobb is a cold-blooded killer, and he has at least twenty equally vicious guards on his property down in Monterrey at all times. You have to let me deal with this my way. When I take the sculptures to Cobb, he'll let Lyla go."

Trent cursed, releasing Marco and walking

away, leaving him lying there on the workbench. After half a dozen steps, he turned around.

"Do you seriously think Cobb is the kind of man who's going to let your sister go after he's kidnapped her and held her prisoner?" Trent asked. "He's going to kill her as soon as he gets what he wants, probably right after he kills you."

Marco sat up on the bench, a man defeated. "I know. But what else can I do? I got her into this. I have to get her out."

Trent stabbed him with a glare. "No. *We* have to get her out. And that starts with you telling me exactly where Lyla is, and finishes with you going to Cobb's place tomorrow night just like he wanted."

Marco looked at him in confusion. "What are you going to do?"

"I'm going to call some friends then we're going down to Monterrey to get Lyla back. I'll kill every one of those SOBs who took her if I have to."

CHAPTER
Ten

"A RE YOU OKAY, LADY?"

At the soft voice near her ear, Lyla jerked awake, bolting upright. Her head spun in protest, and she closed her eyes again, hoping it would go away. When it finally did, she slowly reached up and pressed her fingers to the area above her left temple. It felt like someone had hit her with a hammer.

She cautiously opened her eyes, squinting against the beams of light from the overhead chandelier. Fortunately, the stabbing pain lasted for only a moment this time then receded into a dull throb she could live with.

Lyla looked around, trying to figure out where she was. She was still taking in the distinctive Mexican décor in the living room when she saw the little girl who'd woken her up. Maybe seven or eight years old, she had a cute, cherubic face topped with a wild tangle of pale blond hair and gray-green eyes that were surveying Lyla with an expression of concern.

Lyla smiled at her. "Hello."

The little girl didn't return her greeting. Instead, she regarded Lyla with eyes that seemed far too old for the rest of her face. "Are you seeing fireflies in your head?"

The question caught Lyla off guard. "What?"

"When you close your eyes, do you see little lights flashing on and off behind them? That's what happens to me when I get hit really hard in the head."

Lyla frowned. "Do you get hit in the head a lot?"

"I guess." The girl shrugged. "My dad says I have a thick head and that hitting me is the only way to get me to pay attention."

Lyla's heart broke right there on the spot, and it was all she could do to not reach out and tug the little girl in for a hug. But she didn't know who Lyla was and had no reason to trust her. Pulling her in for a protective hug probably wasn't the best idea.

As Lyla sat there fighting a maternal instinct she'd never known she possessed, she suddenly realized who the little girl was. Heck, who else could she be?

"By any chance, is your name Erika?"

The girl grinned. "Uh-huh. How did you know?"

Lyla's lips curved. "Marco mentioned there might be a little angel down here in Mexico named Erika. And since you look like an angel, I guessed you must be Erika."

The girl's smile broadened, her face lighting up with excitement. "You know Marco? He's my uncle! He takes me out for cheeseburgers and reads me stories at night. He's helping me to learn how to read so I'll be ready to go to school someday."

"Don't you go to school now?" Lyla asked, sure the girl was old enough.

Erika shook her head. "Uncle Marco says I should, but Daddy won't let me." The girl leaned in closer, her voice dropping to a whisper. "Sometimes, I wish Marco was my dad instead of my real father."

Tears stung Lyla's eyes. She was ready to forgive her brother for nearly all the stupid things he'd done in his life because of the kindness he'd shown this little girl.

"My name is Lyla," she said, leaning forward to share the information in a conspiratorial whisper. "Marco is my brother."

That admission must have shocked Erika because she blinked. Lyla took the moment of silence to look around the room, noticing that the big, heavy double doors on the far side of the room were closed. She wondered if they were locked. Probably.

"I guess we're both hostages here, huh?" she asked, turning back to Erika.

The girl eyed her funny. "I don't know what that word means. That's a big word."

Lyla laughed. "It means we're both trapped in this room. How long has Mr. Cobb been keeping you here?"

Instead of clarifying the situation, Lyla's comments made Erika frown.

"I'm not trapped here." The little girl turned to point at a window, which Lyla hadn't realized was open until that moment. "I came in that way. I can go back to my room any time I want. It's where I sleep whenever my daddy brings me here."

Lyla got up and walked over to the window, not at all dizzy now. Then she looked out into the darkness beyond and swayed on her feet. She grabbed the window for support. She couldn't make out all the details, but she saw enough to know they were on the second floor and that the ground below was strewn with boulders and scary-looking landscaping. They had to be at least fifteen or twenty feet above the ground.

"You climbed all the way up here?" she asked, turning to look at Erika in shock.

Erika smiled. "Uh-huh. I like to climb. I'm very good at it. Uncle Archie doesn't like me climbing around his house, but that's because he's a meanie."

Understanding abruptly dawned on Lyla. "Mr. Cobb—Uncle Archie—didn't grab you and bring you down here against your daddy's wishes?"

Erika laughed, skipping over to her. "No. Daddy brings me here when he works for Uncle Archie."

"Is your daddy working for Uncle Archie now?"

The girl nodded. "Yes. He's downstairs talking to him. Uncle Archie and Daddy are both meanies."

"Is Marco a meanie, too?" Lyla asked. "Does he work for Uncle Archie, too?"

Erika shook her head. "No. Marco doesn't like Uncle Archie, but he's nice to me. Well, he makes me eat vegetables sometimes. I don't like vegetables."

Crap. Tim Price and Archie Cobb had been playing her brother. Cobb hadn't grabbed Erika and dragged her off to Mexico against her father's wishes. Tim had lied to Marco about Erika, knowing it would get her brother to do exactly what Cobb wanted.

Lyla was still pondering that revelation when she heard voices coming from the hallway outside the double doors. She thought one of the voices was familiar, but she wasn't sure where she'd heard it before. Erika recognized it, though. Eyes wide, she ran behind the couch and crouched down.

"It's Daddy," she whispered. "Don't tell him I'm here, or he'll beat me good!"

Before Lyla could say anything, the doors opened and Tim Price barged in, a suspicious look in his eyes. Broken Nose was with him, a fresh bandage on his face. Tim looked at Lyla then around the room before he swung his gaze back to her.

"I heard voices in here," he said. "Who were you talking to?"

"Myself," she said. "Who do you think?"

Tim must not have believed her because he came farther into the room, heading straight for the couch. Lyla moved quickly to intercept him.

"How long do you think you can hold me here?" she demanded. "I'm an American citizen. You can't just keep me here."

Price shoved past her and walked around behind the couch, cursing when he saw Ericka. "I told you to stay in your fucking room, you little brat!"

He reached for Erika, but she quickly darted away, running around the other side of the couch to hide behind Lyla.

"Stay the hell away from her!" Lyla ordered.

Price's lips peeled back from his teeth in a sneer as he cocked his fist back and prepared to hit her. "Get the hell out of my way, bitch!"

Lyla put one arm back to make sure Erika stayed safely tucked behind her. She wasn't sure what this act of defiance was going to gain the girl. As soon as Lyla went down, Price was going to start in on his daughter.

"What the hell do you think you're doing?" an angry voice demanded.

Tim stopped in mid-step, jaw tight.

Lyla blinked, stunned to see Marco standing in the doorway.

"Uncle Marco!" Erika exclaimed.

"I've brought the damn sculptures Cobb asked for," Marco said, crossing the room to put himself between Tim and Lyla. "I'm taking my sister and Erika, and we're leaving."

Tim's expression changed, the rage draining slowly away. Lyla wasn't too sure she was thrilled with the malicious look left in its place.

"You brought those damn pieces of twisted metal the boss wanted?" Tim asked. "All of them?"

"All of them," Marco said. "And now that I've seen Erika and my sister are okay here in the living room on the second floor, I don't see any reason to wait around any longer."

Lyla was wondering why her brother was talking so strangely when Tim reached behind his back and came out with a large automatic weapon, pointing it in their direction.

"Now that the boss has what he needs out of you, there's absolutely no reason to keep you around any longer," Tim said. "Or your sister."

Lyla shoved Erika behind her again when the girl tried to see around her then she started easing both of them toward the window. She had no idea what the hell she was going to do when she got there, but hopefully she could get the little girl out of here.

"Daddy," Erika said softly, popping her head out from behind Lyla.

Tim cut her off with a look. "Enough of that daddy shit from you! I should have thrown you out on the street the day I came home from prison. But I'll fix that mistake now, too."

Tim turned his weapon on Erika just as an explosion shook the building. A split second later, the lights went out, plunging the room into total darkness.

Then all hell broke loose.

CHAPTER
Eleven

T HAT'S THE SIGNAL," TRENT ANNOUNCED, LISTENING
to Marco's voice in his radio earpiece.
"Blow the transformer. All Teams move in.
Lyla, Marco, and the kid are on the second level,
right rear of the house. Watch your fire in that
direction."

The signal had been Marco announcing he'd
found Lyla and Erika. Trent had been worried
about Marco keeping it together in a stressful
situation, but so far, he was doing what they
needed him to do.

A moment after Trent gave the word, there
was the distinctive thump of half a dozen blocks
of C-4 plastic explosives going off near the far
side of the dwelling where the transformer that
supplied power to Archie Cobb's entire estate
was located. A second later, every light inside
went out.

Trent and Nash immediately sprang into
action, making a beeline for the house. It was

their job to get Lyla, Marco, and the little girl named Erika out of there. While they were doing that, Dalton and Chasen would lead two other teams, each composed of two CIA SOG operatives. It would be up to them to deal with the army of security guards Cobb employed to protect his residence.

The shooting from the front of the residence as well as the guard complex to the left of it echoed in the night, accompanied by the sharper cracks and booms of concussive hand grenades going off. From a purely number perspective, the SEAL/SOG Teams were seriously overmatched. According to Marco, Cobb had somewhere in the range of thirty-five goons living and working on the compound at any one time. That was a lot of weapons to go up against. But what Trent and the other guys lacked in numbers, they more than made up for in training and discipline. With the element of surprise, and all the lights taken out, he and his Team had the advantage in this fight.

Trent led the way into the house through the back door near the kitchen, moving quickly down the hallway beyond. Right before Marco had given the signal, it had sounded like there was trouble brewing up on the second floor. Trent hadn't heard anything beyond indistinct grunts and mutters since then, but they didn't have time to screw around and get slowed down dealing with bad guys roaming around the house.

As he moved, the infrared emitter on his NVGs and M4 carbines flooded the area ahead of them with light only their goggles could see. But the IR light did its job, making the interior of the house glow bright green in their optics. It was as bright as daylight in here.

They were damn lucky to have any advanced gear for this fight. When he'd first called Chasen to tell him what happened and what he'd hoped his boss would help him do, he'd expected to go in with nothing more than some local weapons they could scrounge up after they'd already slipped across the border into Mexico. He had visions of assaulting Cobb's well-guarded estate with little more than a couple .38 Specials and a salty vocabulary. But assistance had come from the most unlikely source—Joe and his SOG warriors.

Joe and his guys hadn't just helped get Trent, Nash, Chasen, and Dalton across the border into Mexico and down to Monterrey before noon today. They'd also gotten them weapons, NVGs, medic gear for Nash, the communication system they were using, and a complete floor plan of Cobb's estate.

Trent had been more surprised when Joe announced they'd be going in with them to help get Lyla and the others out. Trent couldn't put into words how much he appreciated that. They were in a foreign country, conducting an operation that wasn't authorized by anybody. If things went wrong, they'd all end up in jail for life—or worse. The fact Joe and his men were willing to risk everything for Trent's girlfriend, her brother, and a little girl they didn't know was pretty serious stuff.

As he and Nash entered the huge living room, Trent couldn't help but start a little when they rounded a corner heading toward the stairs and came face to face with a monstrous creature at least five feet high at the shoulder with glowing frigging eyes. Trent almost shot the damn thing before he realized it was a big metal sculpture. One of Marco's pieces that looked like a lion with huge horns and a long tail. Trent vaguely remembered Dana saying something about Cobb buying it. The thing was damn freaky looking in the green glow of the NVGs.

They'd just started moving up the stairs when they heard gunshots coming from the second floor.

Trent took the steps two at a time, Nash on his heels. Please let them not be too late.

When they got to the top of the stairs, they immediately ran toward the room at the end of the hallway. Trent slipped through the open door, instinctively moving to the right to make room for Nash.

The big guy whose nose Trent had busted in Cobb's club was in the middle of the room, clumsily getting to his knees, blood running down his bandaged face while Price was partially hidden behind the leather couch, his weapon pointed at someone near the far end.

Trent stepped to the side and adjusted his weapon to go for a head shot—the only part of the man he could get an angle on—when a blur of movement caught his attention. He had a fraction of a second to see Marco dart across the room as he squeezed the trigger.

Trent's carbine and Price's pistol went off at the exact same time. As Price tumbled to the floor, a third shot rang out. Nash taking out the guy with the bandaged nose. Ignoring them for a moment, Trent hurried toward the couch, fearing what he would find behind it.

Suddenly, the lights came on, the flare of brightness in his NVGs blinding him, and he ripped them off with a curse. Shit, there was a backup generator. That hadn't been part of the intel the SOG guys had provided. This was going to be a problem.

Outside the windows, floodlights started going on all over the huge compound. Within seconds, Dalton and Chasen were calling out instructions to regroup and pull back as the stealth advantage they'd had seconds ago disappeared in a flash.

Trent ignored the radio chatter, dropping his NVGs, and moved around the couch. He stopped cold when he saw the mound of bodies there. Marco was on top, blood spreading from a wound along his lower back. Lyla was curled up tight under her brother, a little girl with blond hair in her arms.

No!

He lunged forward at the same time Marco rolled over with a groan of pain. Nash was immediately at Trent's side, ripping Marco's shirt open to reveal the wound and see how bad it was.

Trent reached for Lyla, his heart seizing when he saw blood covering her right side. Oh God. She'd been hit, too.

But when he touched her, she opened her eyes, staring at him in shock for a second before shoving herself up to hug him.

"I knew you'd come," she said, squeezing so tightly he could barely breath. He'd never felt anything so wonderful in his life. Breathing was overrated anyway.

Trent hugged her back, something that turned out to be more difficult than he would have thought since she was still holding a child enveloped protectively in her left arm.

He pulled away gently, gazing at her and the little girl in her arms in concern. "Are you hurt? Where are you bleeding? Is the kid okay?"

That's when Lyla seemed to realize there was blood on her shirt. She immediately freaked out. Not about herself, but for the kid in her arms.

"Oh God! Erika, are you okay?"

The little girl brushed her hair out of face then looked down seriously at herself before lifting her head. "Yes," she said in a small voice. "Are you okay?"

Lyla opened her mouth to answer, but Trent was already frisking her body, looking for the source of the bloodstains. When he didn't find anything, he breathed a sigh of relief.

"It's not your blood," he said. "It must be Marco's"

Lyla's eyes widened in horror. Both she and the little girl turned to look at Marco, who was facedown on the floor, gritting his teeth in obvious pain as Nash tended to him. Lyla scooted closer to her brother, Erika still clutched tightly to her left hip.

"Oh, Marco," she breathed, reaching out to gently push his dark hair back from his forehead. "What have you done?"

"I got shot protecting you and Erika," he said softly. "After getting you into this, I had to do something. That's why I attacked that big guy with the bandage on his face when the lights went out. I didn't care what happened to me, as long as you and Erika got out of here okay."

Tears rolled down Lyla's cheeks. Beside her, Erika was crying, too.

"How bad is it?" Lyla asked, her gaze going to Nash.

"It's bad," Marco answered before Nash could say anything. "You guys need to get out of here before it's too late. Just leave me here. I'll try to hold them off as long as I can."

More tears rolled down Lyla's face while Erika's bottom lip started trembling like crazy.

Trent looked at Nash. "How bad?"

Nash didn't look up as he ripped away part of Marco's jeans, exposing the back of Marco's bloody leg. "Not too bad, actually. He got hit in the butt, and the bullet bounced off his pelvis and came out his lower back. Not much damage at all."

"I'm not going to die?" Marco asked hesitantly.

"Definitely not," Nash said, reaching into his medic's bag. "After I give you something for the pain, it won't even hurt."

Marco shook his head vehemently. "I can't take anything."

Nash lifted a brow, the syringe poised below the little rubber stopper of the vial of medicine. "You just got a 9mm in the butt. A small needle should be a piece of cake."

"It's not that," Marco said. "I'm a recovering drug addict. I can't risk taking pain meds. I just can't."

"Okay, then," Nash said, putting the syringe and the vial back in his bag. "Moving is going to hurt like hell, but if you're okay with that, it won't cause other damage."

Nash was helping Marco to his feet when Chasen's voice came through Trent's earpiece. "Cowboy, I hope you two have what we came for because it's time to go. The guards are starting to get their crap together and are pushing us back."

Trent looked over at Nash, who was already

up with a shoulder under Marco's arm. His SEAL Teammate gave a nod and moved toward the double doors. Lyla clambered to her feet, Erika still clutched tightly in her arms. The kid looked at Tim Price lying dead on the floor. Lyla reached out and gently turned the girl's face away.

"Don't look back," Lyla whispered softly before nodding at Trent.

"We're on our way downstairs," Trent called over the radio as he moved to the front of their little group. "We'll be out the back door in a few. Be ready to pick us up at the rally point in five minutes."

"Roger that," Chasen said.

Trent quickly moved, leading the way down the hall while covering the stairs ahead of them. It was a good thing he was ready because right then four men armed with automatic weapons ran up the steps.

The men hesitated for a moment, clearly startled at the sight of Trent. It cost them because Trent didn't hesitate at all. He charged at them, firing his M4 on full auto at the same time. It was an insane thing to do, but with Lyla and the others behind him, he didn't have a choice.

Two of the men went down before he

reached them, but then the bolt of his weapon locked back on an empty magazine and he knew he was screwed. He kept going anyway, slamming into the other two men, knocking them backward into another man coming upstairs right behind them. Cobb went flying over the railing, falling with little more than a shout of surprise. The distance to the floor below wasn't that great, and Trent doubted he'd be lucky enough for the fall to kill the asshole.

Before Trent could check, the other two men recovered and got their weapons up and pointed in his general direction. Trent lunged, shoving one guy off balance and tackling the other, knocking him down the steps. Unfortunately, the son of a bitch grabbed hold of Trent, taking him down, too, and they both tumbled and bounced on the stairs.

Trent didn't pay much attention to the fall, mostly because he spent the entire trip trying to beat the hell out of the man grappling with him. Both of them lost their weapons somewhere along the way, so the fight was all fists as they flipped and rolled before coming to a stop on the first landing.

Trent immediately scrambled around and got on top of the man, ready to punch him to death if necessary. But it wasn't. The guy was already dead, his neck twisted around in a seriously anatomically incorrect direction.

Letting out a breath, Trent looked upstairs, wondering where the hell the fourth man was and saw him lying dead on the floor. Lyla and the others hurried past the body and down the steps.

"I probably would have just shot the guy," Nash said, handing Trent's M4 back to him as he walked past with Marco still on his shoulder. "But death by staircase works, too."

Then Lyla was at Trent's side, reaching up to touch his face, her fingers coming away bloody from a cut he must have sustained during the trip downstairs. "Are you okay?"

He nodded. "I'm good. Let's get out of here."

She nodded, following Nash and her brother, Erika clutched tightly in her arms as if the girl was the most valuable thing in the world to her.

Trent looked for Cobb as they got to the bottom. If that bastard was still down here, Trent wouldn't put it past him to shoot them in the back as they left.

But it turned out that wasn't going to be an issue. When they turned toward the back of the house, they found Cobb sprawled on top of Marco's big metal sculpture, the horns of the thing sticking out of the crime boss's chest.

Lyla kept her hand over Erika's face as she scooted past, obviously deciding the kid had seen enough blood and death to last a lifetime. Trent couldn't disagree, though he had to admit Cobb's death had a touch of irony to it.

Fifteen minutes later, Trent and Lyla were in a big Econoline van with the others, heading north on Mexican Federal Highway 85D. Marco was in the back row of seats with the remains of his pants around his ankles as Nash tried to fix him up enough to make sure they didn't have a problem getting through the border stop. Marco was trying to keep his groans of pain to a minimum but was having a hard time. No one gave him any grief, though. Taking a bullet for Lyla and Erika had earned Marco a certain amount of admiration.

Now Trent only hoped the fake passports Joe and his SOG guys had made for Lyla and Erika were as good as the ones they'd made for him, Dalton, Nash, and Chasen, or getting an injured Marco across the border would be the least of their problems.

In the second row of seats, Lyla rested her head on Trent's shoulder, Erika sleeping comfortably in her lap. There hadn't been a whole lot of conversation since the rescue, but that was mostly because there wasn't a whole lot to say. Lyla and Erika were safe. That was all that mattered. Trent was content to simply sit there and hold the two of them for the rest of the trip home.

Lyla lifted her head and looked at him. "Thanks for coming back for us," she whispered.

Trent tightened his arm around her. "Of course, I came back for you. I love you."

She stared up at him with an expression that could only be described as shock. He was confused for a moment, until he realized what he'd just said. Damn, the words had slipped out before he realized it. Probably because it was all he'd been able to think about all day.

"I didn't mean for that to come out this way," he said softly. "I wasn't trying to rush you or anything."

Lyla laughed and lifted a finger to his mouth, shushing him with the tip of one delicate finger. "Stop that. I'm not mad at you for saying you love me since it should have been obvious to me. Why else would a man risk his life to run all the way down to Mexico to rescue a woman he's only been dating for a couple days unless he was in love with her?"

"So, you're okay with me saying it this soon?"

She smiled, tilting her head to kiss him. "Of course, it's okay, since I'm completely in love with you, too."

Trent's heart began beating so fast he almost let out a shout of happiness. That wouldn't have been a very good idea, of course. The guys were going out of their way to give him and Lyla a little privacy, but if he started making a ruckus, they were going to take that as a sign to start ribbing him. He supposed he'd have to be content with simply kissing her for now. But he promised himself that later, when they were alone, he was going to tell Lyla exactly how he felt about her.

He was still kissing her when Erika groaned a little in her sleep. Trent hoped the girl wasn't having nightmares about all the horrible things she'd just seen.

Lyla wrapped her arms around the girl tighter, patting her back and making little sounds of comfort. Erika calmed immediately, relaxing again. Lyla smiled and rested her cheek against the mop of blond hair.

He and Lyla sat for a while in silence,

watching the girl sleep. Erika must have been able to feel their gazes on her because it wasn't long before she stirred, looking up sleepily at both of them. Her eyes soon cleared, taking on an expression sad enough to make Trent nearly cry.

"Daddy's not coming back, is he?" the girl asked in a small voice.

Lyla shook her head. "No, baby. He's not."

A few tears leaked out, but for a girl as young as Erika, she was amazingly strong. "Where am I going to live now? I don't have a mommy anymore."

Lyla gave Trent a questioning look. He knew what she was asking. What the hell could he say to something like that? There was no way he could let this brave little girl disappear into some crazy foster care system. So he smiled and nodded.

Lyla returned his smile then turned to Erika. "You'll live with Trent and me. That's where."

The girl seemed lost for a moment but then smiled before putting her head back down on Lyla's shoulder and going back to sleep.

Trent was a little surprised Erika had gone along with her new living arrangements so easily. Then again, from what Marco said, she'd been handed off from one person to another

for most of her life. She had no other family. Maybe she sensed being with Lyla and him
would be a more permanent thing.

Lyla looked at him. "Are you sure?" she asked
softly.

Trent leaned over and kissed her. "Very
sure."

CHAPTER
Twelve

LYLA STARED AT THE ENGAGEMENT RING ON HER finger for about the thirtieth time that morning. It was probably stupid to wear it while unpacking boxes, but she simply couldn't bring herself to take it off.

It hadn't exactly been a surprise when Trent had asked her to marry him. It had been necessary after the people from the Texas Department of Family and Protective Services had implied it would be much easier to adopt Erika if she and Trent were married, or at last engaged. Trent had dropped down on one knee and put the ring on her finger the very next day. And yes, it had still been romantic as heck.

They'd been working on the adoption paper-work for nearly two months now, and it was all starting to come together. Erika was currently living in temporary foster care with Lyla's parents in San Antonio, but it really looked like she and Trent would be able to bring her out here to San Diego in time for the new school year in late August.

Lyla started stacking dishes into the kitchen cabinet, hearing Trent and a bunch of the guys from his SEAL Team grunting and cursing as they moved the new bedroom set down the narrow hallway leading to the back of their new apartment. Dalton, Nash, and Chasen were there, of course, but so were a lot of other guys from Trent's platoon. They'd been busting their butts all day.

The guys from SEAL Team 5 weren't the only ones. Chasen's girlfriend, Hayley Garner, Logan's girlfriend, Felicia Bradford, and Chief Kurt Travers' wife, Melissa, were there, too, helping Lyla put the softer touches on the new apartment. While Lyla loved the fact that all the guys had come to their aid, she couldn't have done any of it without Melissa and the other women. Some things just needed a woman's hand more than a man's muscles.

Melissa, in particular, was the most amazing woman Lyla had ever met. The wife of the Team's soon-to-be-retired chief had helped Lyla find a job as a teacher in the San Diego Unified School District. Heck, the woman had started the process of getting Erika registered in the same school where Lyla would be teaching even though the adoption paperwork hadn't been finalized yet.

Lyla was digging a stack of salad bowls out of the next box when she felt a pair of big, strong arms wrap around her and squeeze her tight. She snuggled back against Trent, grabbing his arms and refusing to let go.

"The bed is officially set up," he whispered in her ear. "No more sleeping on that crappy inflatable mattress."

Lyla looked over her shoulder to make sure they were alone, then she wiggled her butt against him. "I don't know. I didn't hear you complaining about that air mattress last night. In fact, you seemed pretty happy with it."

Trent slipped a hand down and gave her bottom a light smack. "I'm not saying we have to deflate the air mattress."

She laughed and spun around in his arms, kissing him. God, she loved him like crazy.

"Do you like the way everything's coming together?" he asked.

"Definitely," she told him, nibbling on his lower lip.

In fact, when Lyla stopped and thought about it, she had to admit she couldn't be any happier if she tried. She couldn't imagine how things could be any better. She was getting married to a man she loved with all her heart, they were adopting a child who was the sweetest little thing on the planet, they were all going to Disney World together for a combined family vacation-slash-honeymoon, and her parents were beyond thrilled to finally have a grandchild to spoil—even if they were going to be living in San Diego instead of Texas.

Lyla had managed to handle her first SEAL mission when Trent had gotten a call in the middle of the night and disappeared for three weeks without a word. It had been tough, but she'd done it—with a lot of help from Melissa, the other women, and Trent's SEAL Teammates, too.

Things were going well for Marco, too. Her brother and Dana had gotten back together, mostly because the older woman had seemingly melted when she'd met Erika, completely understanding why Marco had risked everything to save the little girl. What was more, Marco's actions down in Monterrey—when he'd thrown himself in front of a bullet to protect Lyla and Erika—had broken through the years of hostility between her brother and father. The two men were actually talking again for the first time in what seemed like forever.

"Actually, I love the way things are coming

together," she said, kissing Trent harder and running her hand down his chest all the way to his crotch, smiling as he hardened in his jeans.

"I'd tell you two to get a room, but yours isn't ready yet," Nash said from the doorway of the kitchen. "So dump some ice cubes down your jeans, and let's get back to work."

Grinning, Nash turned and left.

Trent took a reluctant step back. "Sorry, babe. Work calls."

Lyla yanked him back in and kissed him again. "Okay, but as soon as we get this place put together and they all leave, your butt is mine."

Trent gave her a wicked grin as he backed toward the door. "Funny. That's the exact same line I was planning to use on you."

With that, he turned and walked away, leaving Lyla to wonder exactly what Trent had in mind for her that evening. Something told her that no matter what it was, she was going to enjoy it.

I hope you enjoyed Trent and Lyla's story!

Want more hunky SEALs?

Check out the other books in the *SEALs of Coronado Series!*

paigetylertheauthor.com/books/#coronado

Sign up for Paige Tyler's New Releases mailing list and get a FREE copy of SEAL of HER DREAMS!

Click here to get started!
www.paigetylertheauthor.com

For more Military Heroes check out my X-OPS
and SWAT Series!

X-OPS
Her Perfect Mate
Her Lone Wolf
Her Wild Hero
Her Fierce Warrior
Her Rogue Alpha
Her True Match
Her Dark Half
Exposed
paigetylertheauthor.com/books/#ops

SWAT (SPECIAL WOLF ALPHA TEAM)
Hungry Like the Wolf
Wolf Trouble
In the Company of Wolves
To Love a Wolf
Wolf Unleashed
Wolf Hunt
Wolf Hunger
Wolf Rising
paigetylertheauthor.com/books/#wolf

ABOUT PAIGE

Paige Tyler is a *New York Times* and *USA Today* Bestselling Author of sexy, romantic suspense and paranormal romance. She and her very own military hero (also known as her husband) live on the beautiful Florida coast with their adorable fur baby (also known as their dog). Paige graduated with a degree in education, but decided to pursue her passion and write books about hunky alpha males and the kick-butt heroines who fall in love with them.

www.paigetylertheauthor.com